With love
John
10.6.2025

Praise for John Seilern's
*Crumbs from the Banquet:*
*A Tale of Six Cities*

"John Seilern has orchestrated a *valse noble et sentimentale* in this vividly personal, and deeply sentient, account of random journeys to several far-flung, diverse cities … their environs, their history, customs, and colour. Take it when going to any one of them, and keep it close at hand." — NICKY HASLAM

"A trip like none other. One would like to join him." — ESTHER VILAR

"I was captivated by this book. It is concise, witty, unusual, honest and excellently contrived. It certainly deserves to succeed." — ALEXANDER WAUGH

"Trieste native and cosmopolitan writer John Seilern brings an eye for absurdity and a respect for ritual to this compelling tour in search of beauty past and present. Blessed with a vast network of relations dotted across the globe, he forms new friendships wherever he goes. A delight to read." — FLORA FRASER

"I couldn't put it down. One of the best travel books I've ever read." — RUPERT EVERETT

"A highly readable account of the travels of a latter-day homme du monde." — PHILIP HOOK

Also by John Seilern

*Crumbs from the Banquet:*
*A Tale of Six Cities*

*Das Gelöbnis*

# Mixed Blessings

## Short Stories

## John Seilern

First published in Great Britain in 2025 by
Tandem Publishing Ltd.

Copyright © John Seilern 2025.

John Seilern has asserted his right under the Copyright, Designs
and Patents Act 1988 to be identified as the author of this work.

Cover photography by the author.

Edited, designed and produced by Tandem Publishing
http://tandempublishing.yolasite.com

ISBN: 978-1-0687613-1-7

10 9 8 7 6 5 4 3 2 1

A CIP catalogue record for this book is available from the
British Library.

Printed and bound in Great Britain by CPI Group (UK) Ltd,
Croydon CR0 4YY.

# Contents

*For my wife and three daughters*

# INVIDIA

## I

My name is Miroslav Kalenitz and my family hails from south Bohemia. I was born on May 2nd 1919. In 1937 my parents died in a car crash, after which I lived with my elder brother at our family seat of Černý Hrádek. In March '39, forced out by Hitler's invasion of Czechoslovakia, we fled to London, where I married a German girl half a decade my senior named Hannah Sturm. In August of that year we set sail for Buenos Aires and arrived on the day after the outbreak of World War Two. I was twenty-one and Hannah twenty-six.

Among the friends we made on our transatlantic passage was the German-Jewish owner of the Excelsior Hotel, who offered us a job at his reception "to make ends meet till you find proper employment." One day I was filling in a form behind the desk when I heard my name being called and looked up into the smiling eyes of my old classmate Jan Janiček, son of our local pharmacist. After greeting me with back-slapping cordiality he invited us to dinner at one of the Italian *trattorie* in vogue at the time. He'd come, he told us over polenta and Chianti, to make his fortune in the New World. Later, on our way home, I remembered mocking him with my aristocratic friends for his snobbery and eagerness to mix with his social betters. The thought caused me a pang of guilt. All that was gone now, swept aside by the great leveller, exile.

Two months later I was hired as a salesman by Maderas de Misiones, the biggest and oldest timber firm in the country. While Hannah remained in the hospitality business – and changed employers twice – I climbed up the ladder to the sort of minor executive post that is the wage of loyalty. Meanwhile we'd kept up with our loved ones as best we could. My own case was simple enough: as an orphan I had no close relatives except my brother Jaroslav in London. Hannah, being Jewish, faced a thornier challenge. Her father, who had sold the family business only to see his takings evaporate in the hyper-inflation of the 1920s, was trying to ride the crest of Hitler's economic boom. One day, after two years of irrepressible optimism, the letters from her family ceased.

After the war Hannah lodged an enquiry with the British Occupation Forces in Hamburg. Their answer dwells with me and always will: on October 19th 1941 her entire clan – parents, siblings, a grandmother, an aunt and an uncle – were deported to the Chelmno concentration camp and gassed on arrival. After dissolving in tears for the best part of an hour, she dried her eyes and said, "Never again do I want to hear about these events. *Nie wieder!* I shall erase them from my mind as if they had never existed, and if ever they come up I shall leave the room." Choking back my own tears I took her in my arms and held her close. "By everything I hold sacred," I said, "and the love we share, I pledge to respect your wishes until my dying day."

For a decade I kept my word, forbidding our friends from discussing the Holocaust, holding them in check if they threatened to do so and diverting any report of Nazi atrocities that risked coming Hannah's way. Still, so tenacious was her sorrow, so painful her wound, that it created a hypersensitivity to political extremism that was to mark our lives in an unexpected way. It harked back to the excommunication of Argentina's strong man, Juan Perón, for legalising abortion and taking up with an underage girl. In response he summoned his supporters to a rally outside the presidential palace, the Casa Rosada. Long enraged by his antics, the army sent a squadron of fighter jets screaming down towards the crowd, killing three hundred activists and wounding many more.

Truth to tell I missed Hannah's reaction to this traumatising event until she came clean a fortnight later. (She'd always been reserved about her feelings.) She'd quit her job, she declared one day at breakfast. "What?" I cried, furrowing my brow. "*Warum denn?*"

"Because I've accepted a position at ESPNA."

"ESPNA?"

"Esperanza Para Niños Abandonados. It's a charity for homeless children that I've been asked to run."

I sat there, silenced by shock. For three years her rise through the ranks of a flourishing hotel chain had dangled the prospect of a lucrative managerial post, equity in the group and a big boost to our lifestyle. "You do realise what you're giving up," I said.

"Of course I do. But it's a move I've been pondering for a while, and the bombing of the Plaza de Mayo pushed me over the edge."

II

One boiling hot day shortly before our twelfth Christmas in Buenos Aires, we left our home on Cinco Esquinas and set off for our favourite restaurant, the Cervecería Munich, to meet a family of *Deutsch-Argentinier* whom we'd recently befriended. As we stood in the doorway their patriarch, an old gentleman with snow-white hair and flawless German, beckoned us over and gestured for me to sit beside him. After a moment of small talk about the previous week's Argentine Grand Prix, our conversation turned to the local gastronomy. At one point I asked him if he knew of an Austrian restaurant in town. "I miss the *Wiener Küche*," I said.

"*Kennst du das ABC?*" he asked.

"Never heard of it."

"Theoretically it's Bavarian but they serve a mean goulash."

"I love goulash. Where is this place?"

"Calle Lavalle. On the corner of Florida."

"That's near my office."

"I know. I'm surprised you haven't come across it." He flicked the ash off his cigarette. "I used to go there all the time but I've gone off it of late."

"Then why are you recommending it?"

"Well the food's as good as ever. It's the customers I object to."

At this point a child's tantrum at the end of the table caused the subject to fall by the wayside. Still, something about the old man's words stayed with me, and when, a couple of days later, Hannah attended ESPNA's Christmas dinner I took a cab to the neighbourhood of San Nicolás. After lingering before a timbered façade that wouldn't have looked amiss in Fürth or Rosenheim, I stepped into a room hung with advertisements for *vinos finos* and posters of King Ludwig's castles. At a free table I placed my order and scanned the other diners: courting couples, men and women out on the town, family groups and a lone drunk-ard at the bar, everything looked perfectly normal.

Suddenly two men came in, gave a nod to the drunk-ard and sat down for a game of cards. At first he merely peered at them with glassy-eyed distaste, but after a while he began mumbling insults. *Nazi Schweine*, he slurred, *Bastarden* and *Massenmörder*, sparking tit-for-tat retorts such as traitor and Jew-lover. At this point a woman bustled in from the street, paid for the man's drinks and steered him outside. By now I'd finished my dinner, so I ordered the bill and enquired as to the fuss. "*Nada especial*," the waiter replied. "He keeps picking fights with those two Germans."

"Over what?"

He shrugged. "Something to do with the war. Every other evening he drinks himself silly till his wife comes to take him away."

"*¿Quien son estos hombres?*" I asked, indicating the card players.

He lowered his voice. "The one on the left is called Klement."

"And the other one?"

"What is this, an interrogation?" he suddenly barked before slapping my change on the table and walking away.

I thought of the incident on my way home. Not only had the waiter's words sounded ominous but the card players' insults had endeared me to the drunk. After work a few days later, I was passing by the ABC when I spotted him through the window; like last time he was lounging at the bar. On a whim I stepped in, sat down beside him and said, "*Guten Abend.*" It was 6.30 and we were the only customers.

"*Woher wissen Sie, dass ich Deutscher bin?*" he asked.

"Because I heard you speak German the other night."

He pointed to the card players' table. "With those low-lifes over there?"

"Exactly."

For a while he studied me, still sober (though not for long), till at length he held out his hand and introduced himself as Oskar Schindler. At my response his eyes lit up. "Kalenitz?" he said. "As in Prince Kalenitz?"

"Exactly. Do you know my family?"

"*Natürlich.* I was born in Zwittau, near your castle of Kalenín. I remember Prince Maximilian, your, what, grandfather?"

I nodded.

"A very kind man. We used to sell him agricultural machinery. I gather he was killed during the war."

I nodded.

For a while he sat there, lost in reminiscence. At last he said, "Do you live in Buenos Aires?"

"I do. I arrived here with my wife on the day after the outbreak of war."

"*Interessant.*" He took a sip of brandy. "Is she Czech too?"

"No, she's from Hamburg. We met in London, where she'd moved after rejecting her family's rose-tinted take on the Nazi regime. Her maiden name is Hannah Sturm."

He furrowed his brow. "You mean Sturm like the publishing house?"

"Exactly. It was founded by her grandfather."

"*Sehr interessant.*"

Eager to return to the subject I had come to discuss, I said, "I couldn't help taking your side in that quarrel the other night. It seemed to me you were being ganged up on."

"That's not quite true," he answered. "It was I who started it. I often do when I'm drunk."

"Who are those two men?"

He downed his brandy and offered me one, which I declined, before ordering another.

"Well?" I said.

He turned to me as if he'd forgotten what we were talking about. "I'm sorry?"

"Who were those men you quarrelled with?"

Slowly he shook his head. "You don't want to know."

"It's funny: when I questioned my waiter the other day he was almost as cagey as you are."

"Then he must have given you the party line: that the thin man is called Klement and the one with the dark hair is unknown."

"More or less. He treated it like an interrogation, but it wasn't that at all." I paused, as one does on the cusp of a momentous statement. "The fact is, my in-laws and their family were murdered by the Nazis."

He looked at me. Though watery and veined with red, his eyes had a gleam of sympathy. After a while he shook his head as if no condolence could do justice to my plight. "Did your wife ever mention a woman named Clara Dorn?" he asked.

"Clara Dorn…" I racked my brain. "I don't think so.

Why?"

His drink arrived; he took a sip and put down his glass; he seemed to be weighing his answer. "Have you ever heard of a man called Amon Goeth?" he said at last.

"No."

"He ran a death camp in Płaszów, Poland. His house overlooked the camp, and whenever he was bored or had nothing to do, he would go to the balcony and shoot some passing prisoner for target practice. Being single, he would host dinners for the surrounding Germans, including myself, and one day he asked me to fetch some wine from the kitchen. While doing so I met one of the inmates he used for such events. The girl's name was Clara Dorn, and I instantly took to her. After dinner she cleared away the coffee, and when she'd gone I praised her looks. Goeth disagreed. 'A Jewess is never pretty,' he said. 'A Jewess is an animal.' Whether he suspected me of the dreaded *Rassenschande*, it must have struck a chord in his evil mind, for on my next visit he asked me once more to get something from the kitchen. Again Clara was there, and while I was chatting to her he appeared in the doorway flanked by his Great Danes, Rolf and Ralf. He was wearing his Tyrolean hat, which always spelt trouble. For a moment he peered at us with a vicious smile. Then he seized Clara by the collar, dragged her into the court-yard and set the hounds on her. Before I could intervene, she'd been torn to shreds."

"*What?*" I cried, gaping.

"Within minutes she'd turned from a beautiful young woman to a mound of blood and guts."

"How *awful!*" Silenced by horror I sat there while

Schindler puffed away on his cigarette.

"By now I'd got to know a little about Clara," he resumed after a moment. "She was an educated girl, a librarian. Before her arrest and deportation she was cataloguing a collection of old books in Hamburg."

A light came on in my mind. "You don't mean the Sturm collection, do you?" I asked.

"Precisely. That's why I asked if her name was familiar to your wife."

"How extraordinary!"

He finished his brandy, ordered another and gave a last pull on his cigarette. "By now most of the books had been sold," he continued, stubbing it out. "The exception was a monastic library bought half a century earlier for the sake of a single work, an illuminated manuscript from the fifteenth century which became the most precious item in the collection. Clara's job was to arrange the items in ascending order of importance. As its rarest item, the manuscript received the highest number and the last page of the catalogue.

"One day the sound of vehicles screeching to a halt led to car doors slamming amid barked orders and stomping boots. When she looked out of the window she saw a squadron of Gestapo approaching the house. Suspecting them of having come to impound the books, she made a split-second decision. Within moments she'd torn out the last page of the catalogue and turned an earlier work into a two-volume set so as to reconcile the list with the total number of items in the collection."

Puzzled, I sat there. "What did she do that for?"

"Because the library had been acquired in a private sale

and was known only to Herr Sturm, your late father-in-law, and Clara herself, both of whom are now dead. *As a result one of the world's most priceless illuminated manuscripts lies hidden in some German vault with no one the wiser of its existence.*"

By now Schindler was getting very drunk, so I thanked him for his openness and went home. In the tram I weighed my options. On the one hand it behoved me to put Hannah in the picture; on the other she might overreact or forbid me from following it up. Worse still, I risked dredging up her suffering for what might prove a wild goose chase. In the end I decided to work from behind the scenes until the need to involve her forced my hand. As I let myself into the flat my mind jumped to Schindler's last words. While getting up to leave, I'd asked him again about the card players. For a moment he scanned me with a glassy eye. Then he shrugged as if to say what the hell. "The one they call Klement is Adolf Eichmann, organiser and avid strategist of the Holocaust," he said. "The handsome one is Doktor Mengele, the Angel of Death."

III

Meanwhile my old schoolfriend Jan Janiček had diversified into a range of industries, including agriculture, insurance, transportation and sport. Such was his flair and appetite for risk that within a decade and a half he'd become leveraged to the hilt, boosting his returns by means of huge loans from the likes of Banco de la Nación, Banco Patagonia, Citibank and the like. He'd always had a collector's bent (before the war he'd focused on art-deco kitsch), and as his wealth grew, so did his passion for the old and modern masters that my family had collected for centuries – hence, perhaps, our regular invitations to Jan's dinners. Afterwards he would point me out like a rare plant, describing me as a "scion of the Habsburg nobility," much to the shame of his wife, the stolid Penelope. At such times I would wonder if he was stressing the change in our circumstances. Whatever the truth, it came to a head one red-hot January morning a decade-and-a-half after our arrival in Argentina.

Having entered a gallery on the Avenida Callao to spend my year-end bonus on a local painting I scoured the usual suspects – Matta, Macció, Torres-Garcia, Leonor Fini, etc. – till I came upon a country dance by the Uruguayan painter Pedro Figari. *Tacuarembó*, it was called, all top hats and checked trousers and polka-dot skirts, and after haggling down the price I went to get the money at my bank. Half an hour later I came back with a bulge in my pocket and a spring in my step to find the item gone, snatched up for the asking price in my absence.

A few days later, at yet another of Jan's dinners, he invited us to admire his latest trophy. As we approached the library I felt a sudden hunch. It proved horribly correct: dominating the room in all its splendour hung no less a masterpiece than *Tacuarembó!* On his way out I was lingering in front of the picture when he turned to me from the doorway and gave me a little wink. Later, in the car, Hannah asked me what the matter was. With a shrug I kept my eyes on the road while she fixed me from the passenger seat. At last I saw her shake her head from the corner of my eye.

Not long thereafter I received a phone call from Jan's

secretary. (In classic upstart mode he was now too grand to call his friends, or at least me, in person.) One of his art counsellors, a German from Hamburg, was coming to dinner the following week, would I like to attend? Ever eager for novelty, I accepted, albeit by myself. (Hannah had a work-related commitment.) The dealer proved to be an expert in German Expressionism called Wolfgang Schreyer; after dinner I joined him at the drinks table and enquired if he dealt in rare books too. "Now and then," he said, pouring himself a glass of whisky.

"In that case you might have heard of the Sturm collection."

"The Sturm collection?" He picked up his glass and gave me a quizzical look. "Wasn't it sold off between the wars?"

"Most of it was, but its rump stayed in the family till it was seized by the Nazis."

He shook his head. "I had no idea."

"I ask because my wife was born Sturm."

"Was she now?" he asked indifferently, sipping on his drink.

"Her father was its last owner and it has great sentimental value to her. So if you come across it, I'd be interested. But mum's the word, I'd like it to be a surprise."

And so things stood, a needle in a haystack thousands of miles across the ocean until 1963, when I was sent to Europe to explore a timber venture with the Czech Ministry of Agriculture. From Prague I rang Herr Schreyer, more as a formality than with any serious hope. Surprised when I identified myself, he said he'd meant to call me but had mislaid my card. When I asked what it was about, he suggested we meet, so we made an appointment in the lobby of the Hotel Vier Jahreszeiten. Next day I flew to Hamburg.

His story proved intriguing. A few months earlier he'd been offered a sixteenth-century Bible, and though he'd stopped dealing in rare books he flipped through it and spotted Ariel Sturm's ex-libris on the inside cover. Was there more where that came from, he asked the dealer to an affirmative reply. At this point in his account he reached into his inside pocket and handed me the man's business card. Bursting with excitement, I thanked and bade him goodbye before hastening to my room to dial the number. A male voice replied, so I introduced myself and repeated Schreyer's story, which he confirmed. When I asked if I could see the items, he agreed.

Next morning he came to fetch me in his car. En route to the outskirts of town I asked him if he owned the books in person, to which he said no, he was representing the daughter of a Nazi official. Half an hour later we reached an old cottage whose living room proved to be chock-full of bric-à-brac, including a bookcase groaning with half-a-dozen vellum-covered tomes. Heart pounding, I pulled them out one by one. To my amazement each one had the ex-libris of Ariel Sturm on its inside cover! After a token negotiation we settled on a price, and by noon I was examining my booty in my hotel room.

In the course of my homework on the golden age of miniature illumination, I had got to know its greatest exponents, the Limbourg brothers, whose masterwork, *De Septem Peccatis Mortiferis* – Of the Seven Deadly Sins – had succumbed to the fire of the Duke of Burgundy's library in 1456. While sifting through my plunder, I came upon a frontispiece showing a nude man with a tongue in the shape of a viper sticking out of his mouth. *Invidia*, it was called, which means jealousy, and as I leafed through its pictures of hellfire and damnation it dawned on me with a thrill bordering on the incredulous that the object in my hands was the sole extant volume of the Limbourg brothers' gem! By the end of the day I'd reserved a seat on the next flight to B.A. and had the books shipped to Buenos Aires apart from their crown jewel, which I placed, wrapped in hotel towels, into my hand luggage.

Fourteen hours the trip took, ample time to rehearse my tête-à-tête with Hannah. As our first mention of her parents in two decades, I had better get it right. Jet-lagged as I was, I waited till morning to come clean. At her sudden pallor when I began, I begged her to hear me out, which she did without moving a muscle. When I was done, she burst into tears, not of anger, as I had feared, but of gratitude. Two days later we took the item to be valued by an expert. The upshot bore out my intuition that it was the world's most valuable illuminated manuscript outside of a museum. When the man laid out the ways of putting it on the market we chose discretion over greed and opted for a private sale.

IV

Looking back, I wonder if the astrologers don't have it right: unbeknownst to me, my stars were lining up with all the malice at their disposal. A couple of days later, at a lunch hosted by Jan Janiček for my company's board of directors – he'd invested in timber and needed their advice – he embarked on a rambling discourse about his collection. As it dragged on, I whispered to my chairman that I had to go back to the office for a meeting when Jan turned to me. *"Serías tan amable de callar tu boca?"* he slurred, his eyes boring into me like the barrels of a double-barrelled shotgun: "Would you be so amiable as to shut your mouth?" Even for him it was a disgraceful insult, too disgraceful to shrug off, so I decided to make some discreet enquiries. It took me a day to bear out my inkling that his malaise stemmed from a simmering extraneous problem. Leveraged to the hilt, unable to pay his debts, he faced the dispossession of his flat and all its contents.

The news reminded me of Hannah's oft-expressed admiration of Jan's beautifully decorated home. She'd always had a penchant for interior design, and here was an opportunity to indulge it. I began by ringing Jan's secretary and asking if I could see him the next day. *Por supuesto*, she said, would 3.30 be suitable, to which I said yes, very suitable, and at the appointed time I was shown into his office. Half an hour later he bustled in with no word of greeting or regret and sat down to flip through some papers on his desk. After a while he looked up with a truculent scowl and asked what he could do for me. "I've come about an offer that might be to your benefit," I replied.

He glanced at his watch. "Shoot."

"You seem pressed for time so I'll be brief."

*"Buena idea."*

"I hear you're selling your flat," I said. (If he wanted brevity, he could have it.)

He looked at me with watery eyes. "Is this a joke?" he said unpleasantly.

"If I've been misinformed, I'm sorry," I purred. "I just

wanted to tell you of a buyer who could take it off your hands with complete discretion. The guy's awash with cash and itching to spend it on—"

"Good for him! You can tell him it's no go. If anything changes, you'll be the first to know." With a curt "And now if you'll excuse me" he buzzed his secretary, so I got up to go. When I reached the door he called my name and I turned around with my hand on the handle. "A word of advice," he said. "Keep out of the adults' ballgame." From then on it was war.

Meanwhile the Book of Envy, as it had been named, had emerged from a slow start, mainly due to the perceived shakiness of its provenance, before picking up speed. The beauty of a small community of specialised buyers is its transparency and ease of access, and within days a bidding war between two parties had shattered the record for an illuminated manuscript by a factor of three to one. A fortnight later, two-and-a-half million dollars reached our Swiss agent to await Hannah's forwarding instructions. Next day my office phone rang. It was Jan sounding drunk despite the early hour. "I've been considering your offer," he slurred. "I'd be interested to know more."

My first instinct was to send him packing but in the end I decided to draw out my retribution. "My friend's been shopping around since you turned him down," I said. "I doubt he's still interested but I can find out."

"Is he familiar with the collection?"

"You haven't exactly kept a low profile," I quipped faux-jocularly.

He ignored the remark. "Who is this guy anyway? Is he for real?"

"A European investor." (Which was true as far as it went.) "I met him on my trip and he asked me to act on his behalf."

"I need to know his name before proceeding."

"That's not going to happen; you'll have to deal with me."

In the pause that followed I could almost hear his blood boil. In the end he controlled himself. "Does he have a price in mind?" he asked.

"Sure he does." The moment had come for the trump card. "But his main concern is discretion."

"That makes two of us," said Jan, plunging into my trap.

There was a moment of silence "Why don't you come and see me in the morning," he suggested at last. "We can talk about—"

"I'm afraid I'm rather busy these days." I paused for effect. "But you could pass by my office at six-thirty, if you like. At that time I should be able to slot you in."

Truth to tell, I had little to do that day, so I spent it in preparing for our meeting. Above all I figured out a price over which I wouldn't go. Having decided to keep Jan waiting I strolled into the conference room an hour late. He looked drawn and tousle-haired with a sweaty upper lip, and when I shook his hand I caught a whiff of booze. After a minute of small-talk we began our parleys. Seeing his determination to stand his ground at a million dollars I hinted at going public, which did the trick. A moment later I saw him out and told my lawyer to draw up the purchase-contract of 23 Calle Luis Aylwin, sixth floor, for half his asking price, $500,000.

Back home I found Hannah fussing over a *milanesa*

in the kitchen, but though my heart swelled with pride at the thunderclap I was about to impart, I waited till after dinner to come clean. As she poured us our coffee, I said I had something to tell her that would make her very happy. She took a sip from her cup and lit a cigarette with seeming indifference. "I met with Jan today," I said, undaunted. "He's selling his flat with all its contents and I've made him an offer he couldn't refuse."

"I'm aware," she said, exhaling coolly.

I knitted my brow. "From whom?"

"Penelope. She rang me earlier. She told me about your proposal." She flicked the ash from her cigarette. "It's not going to work, Miro."

"What are you talking about? It's a done deal. We've shaken hands on it."

"You miss the point," she said with her eyes on me.

"What point?"

"That we haven't got the cash."

I felt a tingle of alarm. "What are you talking about? Half-a-million dollars is a fifth of our net worth. Even after the purchase we can live in the lap of luxury until our dying day."

"No we can't."

"*Was soll das heissen?*"

"It means that I rang Geneva yesterday and gave them the wiring instructions of ESPNA."

"ESPNA?" I parroted, feeling myself go pale.

"Yes. The urchins of Buenos Aires need the money a lot more than we do." She gave me a look bordering on antipathy. "I don't like what you've become, Miro. I don't like it at all."

# V

I seldom go out since our divorce; racked by insomnia, I fall asleep in front of the TV. A month after the events described above, Jan sold his flat for an undisclosed amount. Hannah's status at ESPNA has strengthened since she became its biggest donor. With no children to bind us, we're completely estranged and haven't spoken for six months. At times I wonder if she feels any remorse over the way she treated me. If so, she's never let on. Last night I had a bad dream. I was in a bathroom of the Palais Kalenitz, my grandfather's house in Prague which was bombed at the end of the war. Standing in front of the mirror I opened my mouth to check my tongue when all of a sudden, with the delayed action that intensifies certain nightmares, out came a writhing black viper.

# MIXED BLESSINGS

I

When her engagement to Tino Oliveira came to light, her father reaped endless praise. "Well done!" the wags gushed, pumping his hand for having set her up so splendidly. Behind his back they were less congenial. One day, thinking Thérèse out of earshot, her sharp-tongued great-aunt described the groom's interplay with his birds of paradise as "more like girl-talk than flirtation." She knew the inference: that her marriage was a ploy; that love had nothing to do with it; that she was in it for the money.

Which stung: after all, her liking for gentlemen who prefer gentlemen had been an open secret forever. At first she would question it herself, wondering if there was something wrong with her, but gradually she realised that her flamingos loved her better than the straights ever would; and that the latter's cheery bluster and manly tom-foolery weren't fun. But fun costs money, a lot of it, and when Tino proposed, her acceptance seemed *clair comme bonjour* (in her mother's phrase). Thérèse and Tino, she would mutter, *Tino et Thérèse*, no question, it rolled off the tongue.

Truth to tell she hadn't seen him as husband material until some weeks into their relationship. After a degree in History of Art from the Sorbonne, she'd gone to New York – fled the nest, some called it – to escape the slavery of home and the burden of routine. One day at Tiffany's, where she was temping during the Christmas rush, Tino came flouncing in with his colourful retinue. Intrigued, she rushed to serve him, and as he lavished his beaux with the baubles of their choice he struck her as a soul sister, a potential friend or comrade-in-arms.

At dinner that night, to which he'd invited her on a whim, he opened up about his drinking; his sexual penchants; his overbearing mother; his type-1 diabetes. There was something about him, his candour perhaps, or his boyish figure, or the star-shaped mole under his left eye, she found irresistible. In the weeks to come she became conscious of his snobbery, his fascination with her blue blood, but what did it matter, it happened often, in America it was par for the course. Which left a lone cloud in a clear blue sky: her yearning for children. Afraid of offending him, she waited for a suitable time to broach it. His reply warmed her heart. "Of course we'll have kids!" he exclaimed, kissing her hand with a big smile. "Lots of them!" Later, in moments of soul-searching, she would wonder if her willingness to take him at his word stemmed from honest naïveté or the golden life he offered.

When the time came to draw up the wedding list he asked her to explain the ranking of titles, and on hearing that barons were at the bottom of the pile he struck them all off except for the good-looking. "Nothing but the best," he stated with artless pretension. By now he'd had his assistant alert the paparazzi – "Without the press what would be the point?" – filling them in on every detail of his pre-nuptial party. To his delight they all came, jostling each other at the entrance of the Carlyle, pushing and shoving and flashing their cameras in people's faces, even manhandling the guests inside. *The Post* was there, as were *The Enquirer*, *Veja* from Brazil, the newly launched *People* and the Europeans, of course, among them *Point de Vue*, *Vogue*, *Gente* and *¡Hola!* In total sixteen tabloids descended on the soirée, their presence all the more welcome for Thérèse's annoying insistence that the ceremony proper, scheduled for the next day, be held strictly *en famille*. In the end, eager to make the best of it, he changed his tune, praising his own tact ("Certain things are best played down, it's a question of etiquette") and revelling in the gentlemen's morning coats and the ladies' flowery hats.

Levitating down the aisle on her father's arm, Thérèse held a bouquet of edelweiss flown in from Switzerland, while the groom's permed curls and pink tie might have been tailor-made for the priest's vestments and the neo-gothic flourishes of St Patrick's Cathedral. At the climax of the liturgy the Archbishop of New York raised the host to Almighty God. "*Hoc est enim corpus meum*," he announced, "*hic est calix sanguinis mei*," prompting Tino's ephebes to sway down the aisle, intoxicated by the solemnity of Holy Communion.

Sometimes she would wonder at her husband's fetish for the nobility. Was there ever a greater clash than between his limp-wristed fairies and the stolid chinless wonders he would force her to invite to his parties? Money it wasn't, that was *his* job, no more than wit or good looks, but as they droned on about boar shoots and family trees he would hover around with a blissful smile, unable to join their conversation but happy to be photographed at their side. Which was the very point, that and the gilt-edged guest lists with their dukes and duchesses, lords and ladies and serene highnesses – and even, one magnificent night, an imperial archduke – which he would gaze at for days on end before filing them away and moving on to the next extravaganza.

Their first year went well enough, with trips to Paris and Capri, New York and Salvador de Bahía, where Tino owned a hilltop house named Casa na Colina. Thailand, which he showered with hundreds of thousands of charity dollars a year, was another port of call. One day at a flower show in Bangkok they were introduced to Sirikit, the lovely Queen Consort, who thanked them for their munificence and answered Tino's bow with a regal smile. At her side stood a little orphan boy from the Royal Children's Trust; instinctively Thérèse bent down and kissed him on the cheek, to Her Majesty's visible delight.

That night she touched on her maternal craving for the first time since their engagement. "I don't want to nag, *querido*," she ventured – they were watching TV from their bed at Bangkok's Mandarin Hotel – "but ... the story about babies and storks ... you realise it's a fairy tale don't you?" By now his eyes had glazed over. "The more you insist," he answered, zapping to another channel, "the less it'll happen," causing her heart to contract too painfully for the obvious retort: that far from insisting she'd only mentioned it once before; that as a woman her hopes were natural; and that he'd given her his word. (She knew the answer from her quarrels with Papa. *Plus tu insistes*, he would say, or *n'en parlons plus*, case closed.) In time their quarrels became all the more vicious for his drinking and laxness with his insulin. Afterwards he might leave her a note full of maudlin sentiment and ungrammatical capital letters. "I lay my Apology at your feet," he wrote in one of them, "my Companion on the journey that is called Life."

Then there was his cruel streak. Though she'd witnessed it before – how often had he belittled some hapless hanger-on for an ad-lib comment or improper joke – she'd been spared it so far. One afternoon over lunch at their rented house in Marrakech a discussion of same-sex marriage caused her to turn to the lovebirds on either side of her and quip, "Don't you long to take each other up the aisle?" It took the company a fleeting moment to get the joke; when they did, amid loud guffaws, Tino gazed at her with uncharacteristic sobriety. "You surpass yourself, Terry," he mused, causing one of them to ask if it was her wit that kept them together. "What else?" was his reply. "Her looks perhaps?" In the silence that followed – they were still too much in awe of her to laugh out loud – she realised that the day her banter grew stale her torment would begin in earnest.

Over it all hung the shadow of his powerful family. As chairman of Braçúcar, Brazil's third-biggest producer of bioethanol and sugar, his father oversaw a turnover of fourteen-billion reals a year. Formerly it had been run by Tino's grandmother, and on the day of his twenty-first birthday she'd invited his parents into her office. The matter was sensitive, she ventured, but must be faced. After due consideration the board had decided to settle off Tino by a generous allowance and the use of a couple of houses in return for his renouncement of any claims to the company. When his mother objected to such prejudice

– she might have called it homophobia had the word yet been in vogue – she was told that his leanings had nothing to do with it, it was his flightiness, his indifference to business and the family firm. Tino's response proved typically ambiguous. On the one hand he welcomed the freedom from his family shackles; on the other he chafed at being stripped of his birthright. In the end he vowed to show them that they didn't always run the show. His weapon would be a Bacchanalia of very public flamboyance.

And by God did he indulge it! Torero suits, hussar uniforms, Mandarin tunics, powdered wigs and royal finery, all that glittered was worth a try until it waned. At a photo shoot for *¡Hola!* he dressed up as Louis XIV, the Sun King, complete with a curly wig cascading to the small of his back, a voluminous ermine cloak edged with gold-threaded fleur-de-lys, and the obligatory orb-and-sceptre. For several summers, besotted by all things Teutonic, he took a castle in Bavaria, strutting around in a checked green shirt and hunter's *lederhosen* though he didn't know one end of a gun from the other. None of which helped cure him of his paranoia. On the contrary.

One day a week before his annual holiday – from what, Thérèse would wonder but never ask – his mother came down with a bout of viral pneumonia. It could be dangerous, the doctor warned, even fatal, they'd better come over as soon as possible. What? Tino exclaimed, eyes flashing – and cancel his friends' first-class tickets to Capri for a woman who had never stood by him? When Thérèse tried to coax him – "Mãe is your mother and a loving one at that" – he cried "Horseshit, she threw me to the wolves!" In the end she flew to New York alone. After a fortnight the patient recovered, freeing Thérèse to return to Europe. From Naples she took a taxi to the harbour and a speedboat to Tino's summer seat, as he pompously called the Villa Alhambra on Capri's southern coast. She arrived in mid-afternoon.

For those old enough to recall it, the summer of 1976 was the hottest in living memory. Even the crickets seemed stunned, while the island's fertile fields had turned an arid brown. Bathed in sweat, Thérèse stepped through the front door. The air was cool; the hall scented; the silence complete but for the ticking of a grandfather clock in the corner. Hearing no sign of life, she crossed the marbled floor and followed the passage towards the *salone*. At last she eased the door open – and gasped! Clusters of half-naked boys lounged comatose amid upset bottles of booze, their contents seeping into the furniture. Used syringes littered the tables between bags of white powder and stubbed-out spliffs and cigarette-ends. In the middle, like a debauched oriental grandee, lay her husband, limp, lank dick lolling like a dead snake's head from undone velveteen pants. At the sound of her entrance the group came sluggishly to life. Some raised befuddled heads; others gave her a languid wave; a couple tottered over with mumbled hellos or pecks on the cheek; but most stayed put, greeting her with a blank look or an indifferent nod, including Tino. She noticed his pallor and skinniness and the hollowness of his cheeks, which showed him to have neglected his insulin.

By early evening a veneer of normality had descended on the house: breakfast – so-called, for it was served at three – led to dips in the pool, lounging on the roof terrace and the first of the day's vodkas. Dinner, at 9.30, was picked at with scant gusto apart from the wine, imbibed in enormous quantities. At eleven, jet-lagged and exhausted, Thérèse went to bed, safe in the expectation of the guests' departure next day. In the small hours, awoken by loud guffaws, she threw on her kimono and went to the living room to find a group of Tino's friends lounging about in sultry chit-chat. As she stood in the doorway a French boy who had never masked his distaste for her began fanning his nose. "What's that smell?" he said, prompting Tino to turn to her and drawl, "The scent of a woman, perhaps?" in reference to Italy's recent blockbuster film, *Profumo di donna*.

Back in her room Thérèse threw herself on the bed. Something had happened in her absence, her final exclusion from his all-male world. Not that it was entirely new: for several months now her bons mots had garnered yawns from Tino and his hangers-on, like the flipside to the quip about everyone laughing at the rich man's joke. After a while she nodded off, and when at last she woke up again, the memory of the incident caused a claw to take hold of her gut. While brushing her teeth she remembered a comment by Tino's doctor. "Lack of insulin can produce a condition named diabetic ketoacidosis. It includes vomiting, hyperventilation and a pear-like smell of the breath. Untreated, it can be fatal."

Back in the bedroom the sound of the guests' departure caused her mixed feelings. On the one hand it promised a reconciliation with her husband. On the other, with *ferragosto*, Italy's biggest bank holiday, around the corner, they'd be alone for three days, a risky prospect. Over lunch by herself – Tino seldom got up until mid-afternoon – she asked the cook if any of the servants would be staying on. *No, signora.* Not even the chauffeur? Not until Tuesday morning, was the answer, when he'd be coming to collect them in time for their flight home.

By 2.30 the house lay still. Idly she wondered whether to wake up Tino before deciding against it at the thought of his morning temper. It couldn't go on like this, something was going to give. She picked up her book, *The Omen*, and went to the living room; outside, the sun was beating down like a celestial punishment. At three, his steps muffled by the Moroccan rug, he came in, croaking "I've turned off the air conditioning" with no good morning or greeting of any kind. Tousled and unkempt in his knee-length white dressing gown, he looked worse than ever. When she cited the day's swelter he said, "I don't care, I'm freezing" before stepping out, panting heavily. Presently she joined him in the kitchen, where he was leaning against the open fridge sucking on a tube of condensed milk and a bottle of cheap cooking wine. "You know you shouldn't eat that stuff," she said. "Or drink alcohol first thing after waking up."

"I'm not interested in your opinion," he answered, putting the bottle back in the fridge. Without turning around he stooped to open the cupboard under the sink.

"Have you been neglecting your insulin?" she asked.

"Mind your own fucking business."

So much for their reconciliation, she thought fleetingly. "In the old days you used to thank me for reminding you to take your insulin."

Noisily he fumbled in the locker. "You sound like my

mother," he said to the clatter of displaced pots and pans. "All my life I've been trying to get rid of the bitch and now I've got her clone on my back."

"At least I had the decency to care for her when she was ill."

Abruptly he swivelled around with the words "You fucking cunt!" slurred between clenched teeth. For an instant she wondered what he held in his hand before recognising it as a heavy cast-iron frying pan. His face distorted by hate, he raised it over his shoulder and hurled it at her with astonishing strength. At the sound of it crashing through the window behind her she realised that if she hadn't ducked she'd be dead or mortally injured. And then, suddenly, he collapsed with a stomach-churning groan, spewing vomit all over the floor. While she wondered whether to help him, a whiff of pear drops prompted her to turn around and go to her room. Within half an hour she'd packed her bags and crossed the *piazzetta* towards the afternoon ferry.

## II

He looked young, this detective-investigator Joe Galella, thirty, if that. Earlier she'd been picked up by a police car and driven to the NYPD's 17th precinct, where she was ushered into a room with a table and four chairs. A moment later he came in in a blue shirt and a striped tie. With a token good morning he sat down, opened his notebook and asked if she knew why she'd been summoned. "Of course," she said. "My husband's death."

"How did you find out about it?" he asked.

"Same as you, I guess: from the Italian police."

"When was that?"

"This morning; they rang at four."

After making a note of it, the detective-investigator put down his pen and asked if she'd given her mother-in-law the news, to which she said yes, of course. "Did she blame you?" he said.

"Why would she? I wasn't even there. I told her I believed it was excess glucose. My husband was a type-1 diabetic."

"We know that."

She kept silent.

"The medical report just came in. Mister Oliveira died of…" – he picked up a sheet of paper – "hyperglycaemia. Diabetic ketoacidosis, to be precise." (He enunciated the words like a foreign language.)

"Just as I said: excess glucose."

He put it down, made a note of her last statement and looked up at her. "Are you a doctor, Mrs Oliveira?" he asked.

"No. But I know about my husband's condition. He could be very negligent with his insulin."

"Were you aware that he'd been so in the weeks before his death?"

"I suspected it."

"Didn't you warn him about it?"

"It's complicated." She paused, wondering how much to tell. In the end she merely said, "We were apart for two weeks before I joined him."

"Here in Nu-Yoak, right? Attending to his mother during her illness."

"Yes." (They seemed to know everything.)

There was a pause while he went back to his report.

"The symptoms of diabetic ketoacidosis are pretty clear, it seems. Fatigue, weight loss, heavy breathing—"

"I'm aware of the symptoms of DKA."

"Did he display them when you arrived at Capri?"

"Yes, he did."

"So I ask you again: did you warn him about not taking his insulin?"

"Yes, I did."

"And?"

"He told me to mind my own business."

For a moment the inspector kept his eyes on her. "Did you see your husband die, Mrs Oliveira?"

"No, I did not." Which was true as far as it went.

"It says here that he could have been saved if he'd been treated in time."

"No doubt."

"So by leaving him alone you condemned him to death."

"I reject that interpretation. He had enough insulin to get him through the weekend and more."

"But you knew he wasn't going to take it, didn't you?"

A legal definition crossed her mind: a leading question is a query that encourages the answer wanted. She wasn't going to fall for it. "That, too, I deny," she said. "Though he was erratic about it, he always took it in the end. I had no reason to believe this time would be any different."

In the silence that followed, she wondered if he'd seen through her lie. After a moment he looked up. "Why did you leave your husband's house, Mrs Oliveira?" he asked.

"Because he tried to kill me."

## III

That was three months ago. Shaking her head, she rose from her desk, filled a plastic mug from the mineral-water machine and took it to the window. Without the evidence to back up her claim, the big cast-iron frying pan and the broken window, she might have been in trouble. Odd how they hadn't mentioned the Duty to Rescue, *Non-assistance à personne en danger*, as her mother put it. Maybe they recognised her predicament – that Tino *wanted* to die, that his conduct proved it, and that blaming her for it would be the height of injustice.

She gazed over the smoggy Bangkok skyline. That day *The Nation* had described its pollution as twice the safe limit. Not for the first time she wondered what the hell she was doing there before shaking her head: never look a gift horse in the mouth. All of Tino's assets being owned by the Fundação Oliveira, his death had left her penniless, and without Queen Sirikit's agreement to let her run the Royal Children's Trust "in acknowledgement of your support for the young," she'd have gone back to her hand-to-mouth existence, minus the youth and the joie-de-vivre. Instead she'd got what she wanted: kids in her care; kids she loved and who loved her back. Squeals of laughter drifted in from the corridor. She checked her watch. Twelve noon, the end of the morning lessons. Lunch beckoned.

# Veinte Años

## I

Time heals all wounds, they say, and though largely true, like all clichés, it has its exceptions. Among them is romantic love, which can lie latent for years on end before ambushing one when one least expects it. By my late thirties I had a flat in Pimlico, a job in the City and a steady routine. Every morning I would get up at 7.30, shower and dress and gulp down a cup of tea before driving to the office in time for the start of my working day. Evenings would see me over a TV dinner, a night out with colleagues or friends or a show at the gallery of my classmate Paul Sampson. Since school Paul liked to hobnob with the hip and trendy, and his vernissages would give me a sample of his rarefied social life.

At one such bash I was elbowing my way towards an artwork in the middle of the room when I noted a familiar-looking woman in the crowd. For a while I stood there, agape. It wasn't – it couldn't be! And yet … though no longer the teenager of old, there was no mistaking her olive skin and heavy-lidded eyes and her way of adjusting the tangle she called her hairstyle. As I stood there it dawned on me, incredible and bitter-sweet: before me stood the object of a fixation that had possessed me for twenty years.

We'd met, Keira and I, when we were eighteen. Having devoted my gap year to a trip around the world thanks to my father's generosity, I'd landed in Havana, where I would spend a couple of months before flying on to my next destination. One morning about six weeks into my stay, I spotted a girl having breakfast outside a café near my boarding house. There was a nonchalance about her, an indifference to the glances of passers-by that I found appealing, so I approached and asked if I might join her. Smiling, she pointed to the chair across from hers and watched me sit down.

Taken one by one, her features held little of note. Oval face, full eyebrows, dusky skin, piled-up hair – perhaps it was her curved upper lip that gave her the allure that would entrap me. By revealing her front teeth when her face was at rest, it lent her half-closed eyelids a sexiness all the more erotic for being involuntary. She wore bangles, a gypsy skirt and a Moroccan blouse whose low-cut V-neck gave titillating food for thought. I hailed a waiter and ordered French toast with *café con leche*, after which we got chatting. Irish by her father, Cuban by her mother, she had flown over from Dublin to hear the music of her maternal ancestors in its country of origin. Before we parted she invited me to join her at the Hotel Nacional, where the Buena Vista Social Club were performing that night.

We met at seven. After a while, seeing the hall filling up, we elbowed our way to the front and waited for the curtain to rise. And then, suddenly, to dimming lights and mounting applause the band was easing into *Chan Chan* followed by *Candela, Dos Gardenias, El Carretero, Lagrimas Negras* and the rest of their immortal repertoire. There was something sweet about their Afro-Cuban languor, their fusion of sex and melancholy and old age. At the intro to *Veinte años* I used the crush closing in on us to press my body against Keira's. Later, aroused and excited, I took her to La Floridita, a saloon once used by Hemingway and Graham Greene, where she matched me daiquiri for daiquiri and cigarette for cigarette. By closing time I was tipsy enough to invite her to my room. The upshot merged nervousness on my part – Keira was self-possession itself – with a sort of delicious inevitability. Next day she agreed to join me on my tour of the island. The fortnight to come was to prove the happiest of my life. Varadero, Cienfuegos, Trinidad, Santa Clara, I can still picture the red soil and green sugarcane fields that make up the *guajiro* scenery. Best of all was old Santiago, cradle of *Santería*, the local voodoo, and home to some of the members of Buena Vista. On our last day a black man in a white suit invited us to his house. Under a faded image of the Virgen de la Caridad and a rickety-looking American clock from the 1950s, we drank coffee to the sound of an old radio wheezing in the corner. At one point *Veinte años* came drifting out, the original by Maria Teresa Vera, and when our host cited a restaurant named after the song, we decided to try it for dinner. At eight we took a cab to a village called Bambito, where we followed a narrow alley to a green door marked with the name of the *taverna* in florid hand-painted lettering.

Good food is hard to come by in Cuba, and the Veinte Años proved no exception. A so-so *ropa vieja*, the shred-ded beef that passes for the country's culinary highlight, led to an equally mediocre rice pudding. At ten we were making to go when a stir at the end of the room revealed a six-man band taking the stage. Made up of claves, tres, guitar, piano, congas and bass, they began with the beautiful *Quizás* followed by a string of old Son hits. All the while the singer was eyeing us with particular interest. At one point he huddled up with his guitarist before turning round and pointing at Keira with the words "*Ahora queremos cantar nuestra canción preferida con esta señorita.*"

Coolly, almost as if she'd expected it, Keira crossed the room, all eyes upon her, and stepped onstage. After a moment of swaying to the lilt of the first verse sung by the front man, she took hold of the microphone and intoned the tear-jerking bridge: *Si las cosas que uno quiere / Se pudieran alcanzar / Tú me quisieras lo mismo / Que veinte años atrás.* I remember sitting there, stunned by her voice, her empathy with the lyrics and her way of moving to the beat, and as she lamented the heartbreak of unrequited love it dawned on me with a surge of adoration that this girl, sensual and dusky and eighteen, would never be replaced in my heart.

> *Con que tristeza miramos*
> *Un amor que se nos va*
> *Es un pedazo del alma*
> *Que se arranca sin piedad.*

> (With what sadness do we look on
> When our love has had its day
> It's like a piece of the soul that's
> Torn apart and cast away.)

The memory of those heady days brings back a moment that I ought, with hindsight, to have made more of. On our way back to Havana I'd asked Keira for her surname and she said she didn't have one, she used Keira, nothing more. How so, I pressed, to which she gave a shrug that seemed to say because I feel like it. In retrospect my eagerness to take her at her word may have stemmed from over-confidence in our relationship. Even her vacuous reaction when I invited her to join me on the rest of my world tour failed to raise my suspicion. I would ask her again closer to the date of my departure...

We arrived at 1.00 a.m. and checked into my old room, where we shrugged off the late hour and made love as never before. Having brought me to a string of climaxes unmatched even for her, she lay back in languorous contentment while I fell into something like a coma. At noon I awoke and found her gone. With hindsight I might have figured out the truth by the coldness of the sheets on her side of the bed. Instead, clutching at straws, I kidded myself that she was taking a shower or brushing her teeth. But it wasn't to last: seeing no sign of her suitcase I went to the bathroom at the end of the passage but found it empty. With a pang of alarm I threw on some clothes and hastened downstairs only to find out that she'd checked out, luggage-in-hand, two hours before.

Few things are as obsessive as a sexual *idée fixe*. Like a virus in the bloodstream, it fills every corner of one's being. My immediate instinct was to deny the obvious; she'd gone bric-à-bracking, as she called it, and would come back soon, laden with trinkets; or was visiting the house of Che Guevara or the Museum of the Revolution; or gazing out over the ocean from the embankment promenade, the Malecón. For a while I scoured the streets of Habana Vieja, surprised at her many doppelgängers, particularly from behind. Over lunch at the Bodeguita del Medio I was approached by a busker with a tres, or three-stringed guitar, but when he broke into *Veinte años* I felt a rush of tears and dismissed him with a big tip. Sitting there, my food intact, my eyes brimful, it struck me that I hadn't a single keepsake to remember her by, not even a gift, not even a picture – not even her name!

In the months to come – from Havana I flew to Hanoi followed by Delhi and Cairo – I was reminded of her every minute of the day: her gait, her Irish turns of phrase, her torrid lovemaking and funny way of blinking when she studied the map. One day I was exploring the foothills of north Vietnam on a rented scooter when I came upon a cluster of tourists admiring a big wooden wheel used to irrigate the adjacent paddies. Only after setting off again did the penny drop. By God! I cried out loud, skidding to a halt: she'd been standing in their midst, it was her, I knew it, I'd recognised her from behind! Frenziedly I hastened back as fast as my wheels would roll; mongrels lunged at me with furious yapping as I sped by, but I didn't care. My objective being located at the top of a slippery slope, I dumped my scooter and clambered up on all fours, but when I got there, out of breath and covered in mud, the place was empty, she'd left with her companions.

Back home I spent three years studying Financial Management at King's College, London, and gradually my world tour settled at the back of my mind. After obtaining my degree I joined a firm of chartered accountants in the City, and one night at a do in Notting Hill I met a girl called Cathy, one of those chestnut-haired beauties who belie the cliché of British blondeness. Dinner next day led to a night in her apartment followed by several months of a semblance of love – as I see it now – and when finally we decided to tie the knot, as she called it, we introduced each other to our parents and prepared for the big day. And indeed, all might have gone off without a hitch but for a frighteningly vivid dream ten days before the wedding.

I was following Cathy along a steamy tropical beach. To my left the sea stretched out into the horizon. The air felt close and heavy; dark clouds hung cumbrous and low; the heat seemed like a cloying veil. Suddenly, maddened by lust, I swivelled her around and was making to ravish her when I woke up bathed in sweat, my bedclothes like lead. Only when I turned over on my back did I fathom the truth: that the girl hadn't been Cathy at all but Keira; and that a loveless marriage would be the height of cruelty towards a person who was giving me her life. Over coffee I broke it to her as gently as I could; within half an hour she'd packed her bags and moved out, vowing never to speak to me again.

## II

After that I resumed my bachelor ways: work, the odd film, art shows at Paul Sampson's and dinners with friends or at home. Among them, an annual favour had been granted me by my father when he married his secretary after my mother's death. During their summer cruise through the Mediterranean I could have the run of his house, Marsh Hall in Wiltshire, for my birthday. The thirty-eighth was to be no exception, and a couple of days before the event I was dealing with some last-minute arrangements when the phone rang. It was Paul, my schoolfriend-turned-gallerist, wondering if I would attend his next show. "What show?" I asked with some surprise, for we hadn't spoken in months.

"Jason Spinney. This year's Bond Prize winner."

"Oh yes," I said, recalling the hue and cry over the sculpture that had secured him the award.

"Can you make it?" he pressed.

"When is it?"

"Tomorrow from six-thirty to eight."

"Sure."

"You may be wondering why I'm calling you," he said as if reading my mind. "Let's just say that you're not the sort to let down a friend."

I rang off, puzzled, and looked up Jason Spinney on the internet. Most articles focused on his controversial Bond Prize. "From one day to the next," I read, "upstart Jason Spinney (in the words of the *Standard*) has gone from a name that rings a bell to the art world's darling." After scanning his career – Goldsmith College and a slow start followed by the collection of pots and pans painted monochrome blue that sparked his sudden breakthrough at Frieze – I went over his bizarrely named works: *You're Fucking Joking*; *A Stitch in Time*; *Would That Thou Wouldst Let Me Shag Thee*. Under Personal Life I read, "Spinney's self-avowed heroin addiction ended with marriage in 2005."

When I arrived at the gallery Paul thanked me for coming and pointed out the work that had got Spinney his award. "It's its last public showing until further notice," he said before turning to a famous rock star stepping in behind me. While elbowing my way through the dealers and flashy chicks that make up the contemporary art market, I was halted by a man in a baseball cap chatting to a woman of about my age. For a while I stood there, stupefied, but if I expected a similar reaction when our eyes met, I was disabused. Instead she gave me a little smile as if to say "Oh, there you are" before detaching herself from her interlocutor and coming up to me.

I kissed her on the cheek and stood back to admire her jumbled hair and curved upper lip; her dusky skin and hooded eyes; her gypsy skirt and bangles. Even her face was wrinkle-free, though the contours were finer, the cheekbones more marked, the eyes more knowing yet just as artless. Zombie-like, I heard her say, "It's been a long time," but as I was preparing a suitable reply, a group came trooping between us followed by another. When a man hailed her from the crowd, she leaned forward and said, "This isn't working, Ludo, let me call you in the morning."

The sequel unfolded in a haze of befuddlement. While admiring the famous sculpture, *A Knife is a Knife is a Knife*, I was addressed by another of my classmates, Luke Lewisohn, the third, with Paul Sampson, in our trio of schoolboy troublemakers, who was coming to my birthday party and asked if he could bring his house guests. Having agreed and told him the way to Marsh Hall, I headed for the exit. As I did so, the sight of Jason Spinney chatting to a busty blonde caused me a tingle of recognition, quickly dismissed.

Back home I wondered if there were a link between Paul Sampson's phone call and Keira's presence at the show.

Not that he knew of our liaison, or not from me, it was merely a hunch and an unlikely one at that. Next day my phone rang shortly after I got to the office, but though my heart skipped a beat it was only Paul inviting me to lunch at a nearby restaurant. When I arrived he was waiting for me at the bar, so I sat down beside him and said he looked tired. "We need to talk," he began, ignoring the comment.

"So you said."

He paused as if to gather his thoughts. "I don't know if you're aware but a dealer's relationship with his artists goes far beyond the purely commercial."

I nodded.

"Particularly with the likes of Jason Spinney."

"How so?"

He kept his eyes on me. "Did you see the blonde he was talking to last night?"

"Vaguely."

"Did you identify her?"

I remembered my tingle of recognition. "Not really. Why – should I have?"

"Well … she's gained a certain tabloid notoriety. Her name is Larissa Goraya." He paused as if in wait of a response. "No?"

I shook my head. "Not really."

"She's Russian and new to the job."

"What job?"

"Gold-digging. Of the lowest kind." He fixed me head-on. "She's bleeding him dry, Ludo. And bringing out the worst in him."

I remembered Wikipedia's allusion to his drug problem. "You mean he's fallen off the wagon?"

"Precisely. And it risks killing the goose. He was always erratic, but now he's been fallow for two months. We've had to cancel his next show for lack of material. In my business one good artist pays for all the others, and if Jason drops out I may as well shut the gallery." Our beers came and we each took a long draught. "But there's more," he said, putting down his glass and wiping his lips with the back of his hand.

"What d'you mean?"

"That Larissa's pregnant."

So what, I almost rejoined. Instead, I said, "And what's it got to do with me?"

For a moment he seemed to weigh his words. At last he said, "Let Keira tell you that. She's going to call you later."

I furrowed my brow. "What's Keira got to do with it?"

His look seemed to say *don't make fun of such a serious matter.* When at last he fathomed that I meant it, he said, "Don't you know?"

"Know what?"

"Keira's the wronged wife."

At the office I found a note saying "Keira called," so I rang the indicated number. Her tone was furtive. She needed to see me now, she muttered and I agreed. Within a quarter of an hour I'd cancelled my afternoon appointments and was hastening to the tearoom where we were to meet. When she arrived, I kissed her on both cheeks, heady with her familiar scent. Discreetly made-up and clad in a light summer dress, she seemed to have made an effort for the occasion. "I often think of our time in Cuba," she mused after ordering a pot of mint tea. "Buena Vista and our tour of the island and ... the rest." She kept her eyes on me. "It was sweet."

"Then why did you leave so abruptly?"

"Because I was flying home that morning. In fact I almost missed my plane."

I paused. "You might have said goodbye or left me a note."

"I'm sorry." She looked rueful. "I was flighty in those days. Only later did I realise how much you meant to me. But by then it was too late."

I repressed the urge to pinch myself. "Then why didn't you look for me?" I said. "I'm in the phone book and on Google."

She shrugged. "Marriage, children ... you know, life." Slowly she shook her head. "But when I saw you on Paul's guest list I realised I had to see you." Suddenly her eyes filled with tears. "I'm in trouble, Ludo!"

Her words brought a battery of feelings to my mind: lust and pity; empathy and adoration; hope and the urge to help her. "Tell me," I said.

She wiped her eyes with the heel of her hand. "I was the one who got him off the smack, I who introduced him to Paul Sampson. Without me he'd still be a junkie, a bum!" Her look hardened. "I've seen it before: loyal wives getting ditched on the cusp of their husbands' successes. If he thinks I'm going to bow out while our girls get fleeced by some Russian slut, he can think again." She paused, gagged by anger. "When I'm done, I'll divorce him for adultery. There's no doubt as to the guilty party and I'm going to squeeze him for all he's worth. Then I'll start again with or without another man." She paused once more, perhaps to let her last words sink in. "But first I have to cut the Gordian knot."

"What d'you mean?"

"Prevent the bitch from delivering my husband's child. That's what I mean – and not as in hoping for the best but by rooting out the problem for good and all. Do you follow me?"

"Not yet."

"You will." She gave me an ominous look. "But first let me ask you a few questions." She paused, briefly. "Is it true that you're celebrating your birthday this weekend?"

"Yes."

"At your father's place in Wiltshire, Marsh Hall?"

I looked at her. "Who told you all this?" I said.

"Paul did."

"But … he's not even invited."

"He had it from Luke Lewisohn, your mutual schoolfriend."

I paused. It made sense, there was no denying it. "But how—"

"Who'll be bringing his house guests." A moment passed while she waited for an answer. When none came, she said, "Am I right?"

"Yes."

"And did he tell you their names?"

"No."

"Then let me enlighten you." She kept her eyes on me, no doubt for effect. "Jason Spinney and Larissa Goraya."

### III

By any measure I should have turned down Keira's request. Even if no crime was required of me beyond keeping my front door ajar and leaving my father's loaded rifle on the hall table, the law treats aiding and abetting like the real thing. On the other hand, seldom had Dante's warning about staying neutral in the face of a moral crisis been so unequivocal: there she sat, the love of my life, as innocent a victim as ever drew breath, pleading for my manly support. And then came the clincher. "There are favours that generate a lifetime's obligation," she said, her look solemn. "An unbreakable quid pro quo. If you help me avert ruin and disgrace, I shall never forget it."

That night I found it hard to fall asleep, my mind busy with memories of Keira drinking and chain-smoking at the Floridita; or crooning *Veinte años* in the eponymous restaurant; or her body language and turns of phrase; above all, her adorable lovemaking. Next morning, nervous and underslept, I drove to Marsh Hall to deal with wine and flowers and allocation of guest rooms. As agreed with Keira, I gave Jason and Larissa the suite adjoining the hall so she wouldn't have to penetrate the innards of the house. The guests arrived between six and seven, so I greeted them with kisses for the ladies and back-slaps for the men before taking them to their quarters. After that I went downstairs to prepare a mojito for drinks at 7.30. At eight we trooped next door for a supper of venison and Grand-Marnier soufflé followed by coffee and brandy and cigars.

At midnight the guests began turning in, starting with Larissa, into whose glass I had dropped a strong sleeping draught. At 12.30 I took Jason to my room for a sniff of the cocaine I'd been given by Keira. By the time the last guests had retired, we'd taken another snort, after which I turned up the music so as to muffle the shot that rang out at 2.15 sharp. Only when one of the guests came down to the living room, roused by the noise, did I rush to the scene of the crime in faux surprise, by which time Keira was en route back to London.

For the next seventy-two hours we were kept under house arrest. On the first day I was hauled into the police station for questioning. Though I presumed the interrogator's suspicions rested on my status as the host, they turned out to derive from something I hadn't thought of, namely my fingerprints on the rifle (Keira had worn gloves). Though they made me a prime suspect, I was able to defuse their mistrust by pointing out that the only other prints were those of my father and for the same reason: that we were the only two hunters on the estate. In their cheap suits and nylon shirts the detectives might have been lifted from Agatha Christie. "What was your link to the deceased?" one of them asked.

"I had none," I answered. "I barely knew her."

"Barely knew one of your own guests? What are you talking about?"

"That I had no relationship with her. I met her on the night of the murder."

"Do you make it a habit to invite strangers to your house?"

"Of course not. She came with one of my guests."

"Which one?"

"Jason Spinney."

Though the men had never heard of Jason Spinney, let alone his relationship with Larissa, my testimony made him a person of interest (in the police cliché). In the end we were cleared of suspicion by the endorsement of each other's alibis as well as the guest who had found us in the living room after being woken up by the gunshot. As for Keira, she was aided by an indisputable pair of advantages: one, her daughters' inability to vouch for her doings after she'd put them to bed, and two, the absence of any tell-tale mileage on her car. (With typical diligence she'd used her brother's Mini Cooper, to which she had a key while he was travelling on business.)

In the months to come my mind spun with images of our future together: of our cosy love nest; of dinners out, *à deux* or with friends; of weekends in the country or visits to the cinema. Spring might see us in Tuscany; July on a Greek island; February in the Swiss Alps. When the girls grew up we'd take them to Cuba for old times' sake. For three months we kept a low profile, never meeting or even speaking on the phone for fear of raising suspicion, and when at last I stepped into El Habana, London's premier Cuban restaurant, as it called itself, my heart was racing as it seldom had before.

At the entrance I gave the barman a CD of Buena Vista and told him to put it on when Keira arrived. She came in shortly thereafter, and when she reached my table we kissed to the lilts of *Chan Chan*. Coolly I suggested a daiquiri to go with the music, but she declined, saying, "I don't like daiquiri very much."

"You liked it well enough at La Floridita," I rejoined suggestively.

"La Floridita?"

My answer was aborted by our waiter with the menu. I scanned it and ordered rice and beans while Keira chose *ropa vieja*, the dish we'd had at the tavern where she'd sung *Veinte años* with the band. It was a hint, I said to myself, my heart warming, a token of old times. When the man had gone she gave me a sweet smile. "If you knew how long I've been waiting for this moment," she said, taking my hand in hers.

My heart melted. "Me too. I couldn't—"

"Thank you for putting me back on my feet, Ludo."

I repressed the sting of tears. "Have you started your proceedings against—"

"No words can do justice to your part in healing my family."

I furrowed my brow. A nasty inkling had tainted my blood.

"Thanks to you, Jason and I are back together," she said.

This time I gaped. "But..." I trailed off, too stunned to finish my train of thought. "I thought you were going to divorce him, squeeze him for all his worth, as you put it."

"So did I." She smiled, misty-eyed. "But I love him; I can't help it; and I always will. Thanks to you we're back on track."

Since these events I have often wondered at the coolness of my reaction. Perhaps I'd sensed the moment in advance. Whatever the answer, I felt no welling tears or wounded pride, merely raw hate at getting double-crossed and the need to teach my betrayer the lesson of her life. A saying flashed through my mind: that vengeance is a dish best served cold. "Listen," I purred, raising my index finger when *Veinte años* broke out of the speakers. "Our song."

She tilted her head in incomprehension.

"Don't you remember?" I pressed faux-artlessly. "Buena Vista at the Hotel Nacional, when we swayed to this song as one – or the restaurant near Santiago where you crooned your heart out to its languorous lilts?" I shook my head in seeming bliss. "Twenty years, *veinte años* – the time it took us to get back together again."

Her smile was that of a mother to a silly child.

"We're there, Keira," I gushed, feigning not to have noticed. "We're there after all this time."

"Don't, Ludo," she chided.

"I'm sorry?"

"Ask me anything except—"

"Except what was explicit in our deal?" Still smiling, I shook my head. "An unbreakable quid pro quo, you called it. I bet you were already preparing that lie on your way to our meeting. Or maybe you already had it pat. In any case we both knew what it meant."

There was a long pause, almost as if she were weighing her next words. At last she said, "It's not going to happen, Ludo. I'm sorry."

I shed my smile. "Not as sorry as you'll be when you're sitting behind bars!"

She gave me a blank look. "What?"

"You heard."

"You wouldn't!"

"Watch me."

"You wouldn't!" she repeated.

"It may come as news to you but the penalty for pre-meditated murder is life without parole."

"As it is for aiding and abetting."

"So what? When nothing matters, anything goes." I held up my mobile phone. "If you deny me my rightful reward I shall dial 999 before you've even left this restaurant.

With or without a plea deal I shall disclose every detail of the Unsolved Marsh Hall Murder, as the press has dubbed it – not forgetting to specify who pulled the trigger." At the tremor of her lower lip I felt a surge of fulfilment. "Lots of people lead double lives, Keira. You won't be the first or the last. And if you find it hard to get used to, well, you can always pull out." I paused again, this time for overt effect. "Bearing in mind the consequences."

## IV

An afternoon in January; a duvet of clouds over the Thames; a man lies naked on a hotel bed; a woman in her late thirties steps in and undresses; her full breasts and olive skin cause the man to grow instantly aroused. Naked now, she lies down beside him and kisses him while kneading his hardness. Intercourse ensues, perfunctory but successful. After bringing her to climax he lights a cigarette and observes the smoke drifting towards the ceiling. At last he stubs it out, gets up and puts on his clothes. While doing so it strikes him that no word has been exchanged between them. Dressed now, he glances at the woman from the doorway and says, "Same place same time." As he heads for the lift along the corridor, a song crosses his mind:

> With what sadness do we look on
> When our love has had its day
> It's like a piece of the soul that's
> Torn apart and cast away.

# The Real Thing

*(Translated from the French by André Calame)*

## I

My maternal family hails from Neuchâtel in western Switzerland. Though rooted in the fifteenth century, it wasn't until the early 1940s that we emerged from obscurity thanks to my grandpapa's co-invention of the quartz watch. A decade later, on his way home from a boozy lunch in La Chaux-de-Fonds, he crashed into a speeding eight-wheeler, killing himself and his wife and leaving each of their two daughters a handsome bequest. For my mother the result proved two-edged. Finding herself the object of unwonted male interest, she married a *roué* twenty-six years her senior whose motives fooled no one but herself. One day she received a call from the police: her husband, she heard, had been arraigned for drink-driving in the company of not one, nor two, but three prostitutes. When the curtain fell on my parents' divorce, his debts and her lawyers' fees had had the best of her fortune.

Its balance, which she was forced to sell to finance her lifestyle, consisted of my grandfather's modernist furniture, a world-class collection whose other half had gone to her sister Margot. Aunt Margot has always held a special place in my heart, partly for her feline demeanour, partly for her string of lovers and partly for having sparked my first pang of aesthetic sensibility when she let me sit on a softwood chair with a convex back and brown leather armrests that she called her pride and joy. The moment might be described as the genesis of this story.

Notwithstanding, or perhaps because of, her romantic adventurousness, Aunt Margot never married, thereby shielding her assets from any grasping suitors, among them my father, whose interest she had spurned since long before his marriage to her sister. Shortly after his divorce he came knocking at her door again, and if her first response might have sated his self-esteem, it proved a short-lived affair; after letting him service her for a couple of months she showed him the door. By now he was well into his fifties, and as his success with women waned, his anger at having been done out, as he saw it, of our family fortune, came to settle on his only son.

In a trait he shares with most if not all of his kind, the driving force of my father's character is to blame his every fault or failure on someone else, and while I am unaware of its name in the glossary of psychiatric terms, one might call it the Scapegoat Syndrome. Though I bore no responsibility for the fallout of his divorce, for instance, he viewed my status as Aunt Margot's heir as a brazen assault on his prerogatives. You always count on a malignant narcissist to wheedle his way out of accountability.

Our final interaction took place at the end of my schooldays. Aware of my love of furniture and keen to validate his visitation rights, he would take me around the local antique shops in the hope of garnering my filial approval. One day we came upon a painted cabinet from the Appenzell, one of those masterpieces of peasant art whose value has grown so exponentially in recent years.

Thrilled, I asked the dealer to put it aside while I headed home to consult my mother. An hour later, armed with her permission (and cash), I found it gone, snatched up by my father in my absence. When I rang him, he said he had no idea I cared, bearing out his readiness to double-cross his own son without a second thought. My mother's reaction dwells with me. "Papa thinks only of his material wants," she said. "No more and no less." A month later I came across the item in a gallery, marked up by a hundred per cent.

## II

I was nineteen when I enrolled in Geneva's School of Economics. I remember it as a deadly dull time somewhat alleviated by the galleries of the Vieille Ville and the catalogues of its little auction house, the now-defunct Bourquin, which I would peruse with religious diligence but without the means to act on it. Three years later, degree-in-hand, I accepted a position at the Banque Favre, and one day my boss invited me to a client meeting with a London-based antique dealer named Bruno Camenzind. After going over his account he asked how his business was doing. Too well, Monsieur Camenzind replied, gathering his papers and slipping them into his briefcase. What did he mean, my boss pressed. That he couldn't meet his clients' needs; that demand exceeded supply, causing constant missed opportunities; and that he needed a runner to find him new stock. If we knew or heard of such a man he would be forever grateful.

My first instinct was to put myself up for the job; my next to avoid making any rash moves while I was employed at the bank; and my third to wonder what was wrong with me. There I was, faced with an opportunity as glorious as any I was likely to encounter yet too chicken to grab hold of it? In the end I chose to cut the pear in half, as the French say. First I scoured the bank's client list and wrote down those most likely to possess old family heirlooms; then I spent two or three Saturdays in checking out the galleries of Versoix, Nyon, Morges, Lausanne and Fribourg. At last, armed with my list of prospective customers and new-found expertise, I handed in my notice and rang Bruno Camenzind in Pimlico. No sooner had I accepted his invitation for an interview at his apartment than I booked a flight to Gatwick and sat back with a mixture of satisfaction and nervousness.

After greeting me with matter-of-fact friendliness he began by mentioning a couple of applicants whom he'd rejected "just the other day" for insufficient know-how. ("*Mieux vaut être seul que mal conseillé,*" as he put it.) At this point his phone rang, giving me the chance for a discreet once-over of his living room. When at last he hung up, I pointed out a chair with pigskin armrests and a sleek design and asked if it was Danish. Indeed it was, he said. "By Hedin Holm?" I pressed with a knowing look, at which he shook his head and answered, "Believe me, whoever gets me a Hedin Holm will be a made man. He's the greatest furniture maker of all time." For a while we discussed Holm's masterpiece, the Geronimo chair, which had disappeared during the war and was valued, *in absentia* so to speak, at between six- and eight-million dollars, "far short of its true worth given its rarity and aesthetic perfection." When we got down to the interview proper he asked which art movement most influenced the Louis XIII style. "Italian Mannerism," I replied.

"How come?"

"Because the Queen Mother was Florentine."

"What was her name?"

"Marie de Medici."

"What about Empire? What foreshadowed and what followed it?"

"Directoire and Biedermeier."

"And what was its greatest influence?"

"Classical Rome."

"Anything else?"

"Yes, ancient Egypt."

"Very good." He nodded, perhaps impressed by my rapid-fire answers. "And now for something a little more modern. To what does Gio Ponti owe his style?" Inferring it to be a movement rather than a person, I suggested the Viennese Secession, which caused him to shake his head with a hint of impatience and say *mais non*, it was the Novecento Italiano. And so it went, query after query most of which I knew the answers to though he caught me out a couple of times (among them, to my shame, on Wegner's Knibtangstol).

When he was done, he sat back as if harbouring a further point. "What is it that attracts you to the antiques trade?" he said at last.

For a moment I sat there. My response deserved careful thought. "Beauty," I said at last. "As well as artistry and patina and … history." My heartbeat quickened. "Nothing gives me greater joy than a bed from the court of Louis XIV or Carlyle's desk later acquired by Oscar Wilde or …

I don't know, an old Bohemian chandelier." Even before I had finished my explanation he was shaking his head. "No, no," he said. "You're missing the point. You're not here to indulge your fancies or put together a collection but to make money, as much and as quickly as you can – for both of us. Business is business and don't ever forget it." With these words he offered me a two-month retainer to be deducted from future sales.

Out on the street I checked my watch and realised I had ample time to visit the local shops before my return flight. Within minutes I was trooping through the Ali Baba's caves of Pimlico – Adam Bain, Le Grand Siècle, Dorian Gray, Nicky Haslam, etc. – each more stylish, each more amazing than the last. The last had a stack of complimentary *Antiquarian Digest*s by the entrance, so I picked one up and flipped it open on my way to the airport. 'Confessions of an Anonymous Runner', said its leading article, and within seconds I was absorbed in it with growing fascination. At first he played it straight, he wrote, buying and selling at even-handed margins, but after a while he became aware of certain tricks of the trade, the most devious of which he described in detail. When calling on a potential seller he would come with a so-called specialist. At first the latter kept quiet. Only when hands were about to be shaken, would he step forward, clear his throat and draw attention to an identical piece recently sold for half the price. The ruse worked nine times out of ten. Perturbed, I folded the magazine and looked out of the window. Was this what I'd got myself into? Was fraud an inherent part of my vocation? There and then I decided to avoid such double-dealing even if it cost me the odd coup.

I shall never forget my first opportunity. It happened a fortnight later: while leafing through the catalogue of Bourquin's next sale I came across a Louis XVI card table described as *Table de jeux française, sans doute fin XVIII^{ème}*. Endowed with the magical term *non-attribué* it was valued at 1,000 to 1,300 Swiss francs. Eager to prove my worth, I went to Bourquin's showroom and scrutinised the piece from every angle – the patina; the chess-board surface worthy of Marie-Antoinette or one of her ladies-in-waiting; the tapering legs that were to inspire Jacques Adnet and Jean-Michel Frank a century-and-a-half later. At last it struck me – of course! How could I have been so dense? It was an Étienne Janssen from the late 1770s! In the days to come I rang various other auction houses and scanned my old catalogues for Janssen's most recent results. In the end I alighted on a gross market value of 10,000 Swiss francs before deducting Camenzind's margin and my own and ending up with a third of that sum.

On the big day I sat down at the back of the auction room determined to keep to my limit of 3,300 francs. Never having bid before, I marvelled at the speed of the process: by 2,500 a lone buyer remained, so I raised my hand for the first time. Two-six; two-seven; two-eight; two-nine – at 3,000 my rival bowed out, giving me the buzz of ownership that was to thrill me so often in the years to come. Next morning I hastened to pick up my booty. Having dusted and polished it as best I could, I awaited Camenzind's visit to Geneva ten days hence.

I remember the moment he stepped into my storage room. He began by scrutinising the object from every angle while I stood there, my heart thumping fit to rupture my rib cage; studiously he turned it around and checked its underside with a magnifying glass; at last he put it down and looked at me. That's no Janssen, he said with no trace of a smile. Why not? I stammered. Simple: though the wood seemed of a suitable age, perhaps lifted from the panelling of an old house, and the artistry adequate, the fastenings betrayed recent manufacture. To prove his point he showed me the dovetailing and screws, machine-made for the one and mass-produced for the other. Worse still, the lack of a stamp, the intertwined EJ so typical of the artist's work, revealed the piece to be either a clever imitation or a brazen forgery.

For a while I toyed with the idea of selling it, if not as a Janssen, at least as an eighteenth-century original. Three-thousand francs meant a lot to me at the time, and I saw no reason to give it up for a principle disregarded by so many in my trade. In the end I recalled my vow to avoid such deceit even if it cost me the odd coup. To this day the table stands in a corner of my living room, a beautiful if worthless memento of my beginner's naïveté and the code of ethics that had prevented me from stooping to the level of those less honourable than I.

If the lesson dwelled with me as one of the most important of my career, my success in later years derived less from my failures – of which there were a few more, though none as bad as the first – than from the era's business climate, a sort of last hurrah before the arrival of the internet. From experts to amateurs, from widows to divorcées and from town houses to *maisons villageoises*, limitless was the merchandise across western Switzerland. Soon I was venturing into France, once as far as Lyon, and with a never-ending supply and Camenzind's keen appetite, I seemed to have struck gold. And indeed, were it not for my tendency to treat the future like a mirage on a desert highway I might have provided for a rainy day.

But I didn't, and while my competitors were creating their own websites, each slicker than the last, I continued to live in the past, hosting slap-up dinners at the best restaurants in town or taking my girlfriends to the gambling tables of Monte Carlo. Which recalls a line by Hemingway: that bankruptcy comes gradually, then suddenly, and one day I awoke to the chilling realisation that my future had gone the way of my cash. To make matters worse I had made a down-payment on a house in Geneva's most exclusive district of Cologny with the balance to be handed over as soon as the sellers found a new home.

## III

During the years of plenty my mind had often turned to my Aunt Margot. Unlike her sister's her collection must be intact, I thought, but apart from her living room, with its Royère armchairs and Diego Giacometti lamp, I had never seen the rest of her apartment. Such was the backdrop to my weekly lunch at Maman's shortly after the events described above. Out of the blue she told me that Aunt Margot was ill. "Is that so?" I mumbled between mouthfuls, presuming her to have caught the 'flu going around.

"Yes, her days are numbered."

"*What?*" I turned to her with my fork in mid-air. "What do you mean?"

"Just that. Last week she collapsed in the street and was taken to hospital. The diagnosis came this morning." Her voice wavered audibly. "It's leukaemia, acute rather than chronic and all the more inexorable."

For a moment I sat there, my shock worsened by my mother's emotion. "Should I pay her a visit?" I said at last.

"I'm sure she'd be happy to see you," she replied. "But beware of Papa's machinations."

"What machinations?"

"He's been denouncing your career as glorified theft."

I felt a tingle down my spine. "D'you mean he's trying to…" I trailed off, loath to complete my train of thought.

"Supplant you in her will? So it would seem. Being single and childless Margot is free to leave her assets to whomever she pleases. Never forget what I told you. Self-interest is your father's only driving force. Nothing else matters."

Two days later I went to see the patient. Surrounded by her artworks, which I made sure not to scrutinise too openly, she greeted me from her couch. Though thinner than I remembered her, her weight loss added to her elegance. After thanking her for letting me come, I enquired after her health. "*Ça va,*" she said. "Though I have no illusion about my fate. It's not fun, *mais c'est la vie.*" When I offered to make tea, she accepted, after which we chatted about family and friends and the stock markets and world affairs. Presently I sensed her to be tiring and bade her adieu. On my way downstairs I heard footsteps coming up. Suddenly suspicious, I hid in a recess of the lower landing, and after a moment the tinkle of a doorbell caused me to peep through the banister to the sight of my father on Aunt Margot's doorstep, waiting to be let in.

In the months to come I would call on her twice a week, sometimes more. Our discussions veered from the usual platitudes – the weather; the latest TV shows; mutual acquaintances – to the French elections, the trial of O. J. Simpson or the Bosnian war. Only one thing remained out of bounds: my father, fuelling my paranoia at the venom he must be planting in her mind. One day, as if seeing through me, she enquired after my career. My reply, that I'd seen better days, prompted a look of empathy, or so I thought. Her Mona-Lisa smile made more mysterious by her pallor, she asked if it was she who had sparked my love of antiques. "You mean by letting me sit on that Danish chair as a child?" I asked. When she nodded, I said, "Yes, it was. In fact…" – my voice wavered – "you changed my life."

Shortly afterwards she took a turn for the worse. I'd seen it coming, of course, and when she was moved to a hospice it came as no surprise. As usual she was well organised: loath to waste money on storage and insurance she'd left her best pieces in her sister's care. A few days later I went to my mother's flat for our weekly lunch. I forget whether I gasped out loud as I stepped in: ensconced in the hall, its fittings in perfect condition, stood the armchair Aunt Margot had let me sit on those many years ago! For a while I stood there in astonishment: the softwood frame; the brown leather arms; the cow-horn back later to inspire Hans Wegner. It couldn't be but it was – the sole extant Geronimo, Hedin Holm's lost masterpiece and the most sought-after piece of furniture on earth!

My first reaction was to stand there, dazed by bafflement

and disbelief. And my second to remember Bruno Camenzind describing its rarity and aesthetic perfection and estimating its value at between six- and eight-million dollars. And then, to top it off as if the stars had lined up to deal me an immutable clincher, a message from my estate agent awaited me at home. The sellers of my putative house in Cologny had unearthed a new home and wished to exchange in forty-eight hours.

My first instinct was to pour myself a strong whisky and then another. My second to postpone the deadline by a month (which I did the next day); and my third that I could no more afford to lose my down-payment than to pay for the balance of the property. As I stood there I recalled a Florentine forger who worked from high-definition photographs but whom I'd never used given my vow to avoid the double-dealing laid out in the *Antiquarian Digest*. Shrugging off such piety as blindsided by events, I hatched a plan, and two days later I landed at Peretola airport armed with the requisite pictures and the item's dimensions to the last millimetre.

No sooner had I checked into my *pensione* near the church of Santa Trinita than I crossed the eponymous bridge and proceeded to the alley off the Piazza del Carmine that housed the forger's studio. While watching him inspect the photos with a magnifying glass, I suggested a deadline so tight that I thought he would refuse. But he didn't; instead he gave a nod of assent. Back at my hotel I called Bruno Camenzind, who reacted to my story with due stupefaction. Was I certain it was real, he asked when he found his voice, perhaps in reference to the Janssen affair; in reply I assured him I'd learned my lesson and could tell a genuine from a fake. When I described the provenance under the seal of the strictest secrecy, he asked if there was a sales contract among my grandfather's effects, to which I said no, perhaps because the item had come into his hands during the war.

After hanging up, I sent him the pictures by express courier. Two days later he rang up to ask for my price, so I said four-million dollars plus a strict non-disclosure agreement and the pledge to dispose of it in a private sale. (Though he may have wondered at my resolve, he didn't let on, no doubt unwilling to risk so incredible an opportunity.) Three days before the deadline of my house in Cologny I drove to Florence to collect the chair and take it to Switzerland via the small, unmanned border crossing of Pointe de Barasson.

Next morning I parked my van outside my mother's block of flats and waited for her to come out for her daily constitutional. No sooner had she disappeared down the street than I hastened upstairs and swapped my Geronimo with the fake one. At my storeroom I handed Camenzind the real thing after a nail-biting but ultimately satisfactory inspection. Two weeks later I rang him up and asked if he'd sold it. Indeed he had, he said. For how much? I said, my palms dampening. After a brief hesitation he said seventeen-million dollars, twice its market estimate. I remember sitting there after hanging up. If I'd disposed of it myself I would have made four times what I did. In the end I shrugged my shoulders and vowed not to cry over spilled milk.

## IV

A fortnight later, a month after Aunt Margot's admission to the hospice, the graphs above her bed flattened out. It was a painless death, like a drift into the beyond, and the next few days kept us busy with the funeral. Forty-eight hours after the ceremony I was summoned for the opening of her will. At the sight of my father sitting smugly in the lawyer's office, I congratulated myself on my foresight. After disposing of the small talk, the man unsealed an envelope and turned to him. "*Cette lettre est addressée à vous, monsieur,*" he said, causing my palms to dampen. "*Cher André,*" he read out loud after putting on his glasses.

"Though the memories you provided me never lived up to your vanity and greed, I don't want to cut you off completely. So I have decided to leave you your favourite snapshot of me, the one in the short red dress. The rest of my estate I leave in its entirety to the charities listed on the attached schedule apart from the chair by Hedin Holm known as Geronimo, which I leave to your son, my only nephew, in memory of the episode that inspired his love of furniture."

In the taxi I pictured myself tendering my heirloom for valuation. The materials looked fine, the expert would concede, no doubt with a rueful air, and the artistry too. Sadly the fastenings were of recent manufacture…

# Whispering Gallery

I

I awoke. No light pierced the darkness, not even a glint, I might as well have been blindfolded. At last I remembered where I was: the Caravaggio room, named after the painter said to have used it in the early seventeenth century. Three-thirty, said my watch's fluorescent hands. I felt for Valeria and found her gone; the sheets were cold on her side of the bed; she must be feeding the baby, I thought, turning over on my back.

Presently a dim shaft of light appeared under the door: the moon must have come out over the castle. Maybe a pee would help me go back to sleep, I thought, feeling for the switch, but when I pressed it, the bulb popped. Damn! I cried out loud. After a momentary confusion I got up, felt my way to the bathroom and did what I had come for. And then, while making my way back to the bed, I heard a whisper in the corner of the room. "Don't," a voice was pleading from beyond the wall, so I drew nearer and heard it again, more pressingly – "Please don't!" – though this time it fused into a sigh of pleasure. With a tingle of disquiet I slipped into my dressing gown and stepped out into the corridor.

Zombie-like I crept down the passage and turned right and right again towards the room from which the sound had come. The vision that met me when I opened the door stopped me dead in my tracks: pallidly lit by the moon, naked as the day they were born, my wife and her brother were locked in a sexual embrace at the foot of the whispering gallery. For a while I stood there, reeling with odium and disbelief. At last I rushed back to my room, threw on my clothes and lurched downstairs and across the courtyard. A minute later I was driving into the dawn as fast as my wheels would roll.

## II

London, another hot morning; as I sit in the kitchen my coffee bubbles up in the *caffettiera*, a birthday present from my classmate at university, Rodolfo Barbarigo. I recall our first meeting: I, pasty-faced and flaxen-haired, spawn of the English middle class; he, ethereal and dusky, scion of Italian nobility. In addition to their Venetian palazzo, his family had a thirteenth-century pile in southern Italy called Castello di Giordano, which they used as a summer retreat. As the weeks passed, Rodolfo and I would often go out for a drink or a cup of tea to discuss our common interests. From Titian to Turner, from Bach to Beethoven, from Proust to Pushkin we were made to be friends.

I remember my first visit to his room. Two photographs stood on his bedside table. The first I deduced to be of his parents; the second showed a very pretty girl with chestnut hair. "Who's the beauty?" I asked, picking it up. Stony-faced, he took it off me and put it back where it belonged. "That's my sister Valeria," he said unsmilingly. Seeing his unease, I tried to lighten the mood but to no avail. On my way out I caught sight of a letter on his desk, illegible but for a phrase in capital letters: "*TROVACI QUALCUNO DI ADATTO,*" it said – find us someone suitable – signed

Mamma. How different my fate would have turned out if I'd known what it meant! But I didn't, nor did I enquire; it was none of my business anyway.

One day Rodolfo told me that an ancestor of his had sheltered Caravaggio from a homosexual imbroglio that risked destroying his career. Was there any evidence of it? I asked. Not really, he replied, it was mainly word of mouth, though an account of it was said to be stored in the library of the castle. Said to be? I pressed: what did he mean? That it had disappeared, was his answer, vanished without a trace. "You could try and unearth it to kick-start your career." Exhilarated by the invitation, I agreed: what could be more exciting for a budding art historian than to bring to light a long-lost scandal about one of our greatest painters? A week after my finals I landed at Benevento, rented an ancient Fiat 500 and rattled off towards the castle of Giordano.

An hour later I got out of the car and lingered at the bottom of the path. Above me a jumble of turrets and ramparts rose higgledy-piggledy into the blue. After a while I picked up my bag and followed the dirt track that led towards the house. As I approached the entrance, the girl from Rodolfo's photograph appeared in the doorway. "You must be Ashley," she said, holding out her hand and squinting into the sun. Tanned and creamy-skinned, she looked even prettier in real life. As we shook hands she added, "And I'm Valeria." A moment later she showed me to my room before stepping out with a breezy "Lunch is at 1.30." As she shut the door I recalled an old song. "Do you believe in a love at first sight? Yes I'm certain that it happens all the time..."

Over drinks in the *salone* I met the count and countess, elegant and welcoming, though the count looked unwell. The furniture was mainly Venetian, in line with the owners' roots. Looking back, I wonder if I noticed a change in Rodolfo's attitude, a certain coldness behind his offer of a drink. As for the hosts, they treated me like a friend, chatting away with an openness perhaps emboldened by my passable Italian. We talked of this and that: President Leone; the terrible heatwave; an earthquake in Sicily; a spike in Italy's rate of abortion, which the contessa called desperately sad. At one point she cited a note discovered among the effects of her husband's late great-grandmother alluding to *il racconto della visita di Caravaggio depositato nella grande biblioteca.*

The library was a spacious room with dark-wood bookcases curving inwards under a frescoed ceiling of frolicsome putti peeping out of bouffant clouds. A jumble of volumes and papers was arranged, if such is the word for the chaos around me, by subject-matter and date. After giving me the lie of the land as best he could, Rodolfo left me to my devices with a cheerful "Good luck." For several minutes I stood there, stifled by the heat, wondering where to begin. After a while I spotted a ladder in the corner of the room and slid it along its rail to a shelf captioned *Miscellanea Sec. XVI-XVII.*

I climbed to the top, opened the lattice screen and began sifting through the works behind it. Greek treatises vied with illuminated manuscripts, mediaeval maps and even a Coptic bible – everything except the item I was looking for. Fleetingly I thought of consulting Valeria before shrugging it off as a lust-driven distraction. Instead

I climbed back down the ladder to think up a plan of action. As I stood there bathed in sweat, the door suddenly opened to reveal the object of my thoughts with a bottle of San Pellegrino and two glasses on a tray. "Knowing the heat in this room I thought you'd like some refreshment," she said, stooping to deposit her load on the table.

I smiled. "How nice of you," I said, meaning it. For the first time I thought she liked me too.

"How are you getting on?" she asked.

"Like a hippopotamus looking for a pea," I said.

Laughing, she poured me a glass. Lit by a shaft of sunlight, specks of dust hovered in the air behind her.

"Do *you* have any idea where the item might be?" I pressed, taking a sip and wrapping my hands around the icy crystal.

"None at all." She sat down and so did I. "But I can tell you all about it."

"I'm all ears."

"Legend has it that in 1602 Caravaggio was caught *in flagrante* with Cardinal Barbarigo, owner of this house."

"I thought cardinals were celibate."

She tilted her head as if to say if you believe that you'll believe anything. "Afraid of the scandal going public, my ancestor gave him refuge until it had died down," she said without addressing my comment.

"It all sounds very vague."

"With good reason."

"Why?"

She took a sip of water and wiped her lips with the back of her hand. "Because it's nonsense," she said.

"But…" I furrowed my brow. "Rodolfo claimed it was

common knowledge."

"More like wishful thinking."

"Has no one looked into it?"

"Not outside the family. The experts aren't interested. They see it as an old wives' tale kept up by the likes of my brother."

"What about your great-great-grandmother's note? The one your mother mentioned at lunch."

"That's hot air too. It was 'mislaid' after her death and never found. The whole thing's a cock-and-bull story based on the most tenuous word-of-mouth."

A fly buzzed against the window; grids of sunlight criss-crossed the floor; the heat bore down like a physical load. "I don't buy it," I said, wiping a drop of sweat from my brow. "Where there's smoke there's fire."

"In that case let me at least point you in a plausible direction." She got up and slid the ladder under a plaque saying Cardinale Giovanni. "Focusing on the sixteenth century in general, as you just did, is a waste of time. If the scandal was hushed up it would hardly feature in any public chronicle of the day. Far more promising is the diary of Cardinal Giovanni. Unfortunately it was damaged by fire in 1857. What's left is said to be written in an impenetrable code."

"What kind of code?"

"Some obscure cipher in the Gothic script."

"Interesting." I paused, my mind a jumble of questions. "Has your father seen it?"

"No. My father has no interest in his ancestry. He collects guns and motorcars. Caravaggio, to him, is a Corvette of the same name." She emptied her glass. "The last person supposed to have seen it was my great-uncle, who died six years ago. As a student he was gripped by the same virus as you. In the end, unable to crack the code, he gave up."

"You mean he found the cardinal's diary?"

"So he claimed."

"And shelved it God knows where?" I said, gloomily completing her train of thought.

"Exactly." Suddenly she smiled. "Cheer up! Persistence will overcome resistance."

"Persistence is no guarantee of success," I retorted.

"Maybe not, but its absence is a guarantee of failure."

Today the moment strikes me as my first conscious realisation of Valeria's precocious mind. I say conscious for it must have struck me by then. Even when we met she exuded an intelligence as artless as it was attractive. For intelligent she was, astonishingly so, with a poise and *savoir-faire* well beyond her age.

### III

In the days to come, I acquired a steady routine. After breakfast with the count (the countess had hers in her room while Rodolfo and Valeria invariably slept in) I would resume my work where I'd left off the day before. Having found nothing of note under Cardinal Giovanni, I began again from scratch, scouring the categories in chronological order: the Gothic, the Renaissance, Mannerism, Baroque, Family History and Miscellania (by century). After lunch another bout of work might include a visit from Valeria with the usual bottle of San Pellegrino. When he felt well enough, the count might take me to see his collections of weapons, which he kept in an unlocked cupboard in his study (somewhat to my surprise). Sunset might see us in the village for a *caffè gelato* with Rodolfo or his sister or both. A nearby monastery had a famous crucifix and pictures by Perinetto.

Two things strike me when I think of those heady days. First that my feelings for Valeria grew into something like a fixation. And second that Rodolfo had become morose, to his sister's evident disquiet, almost as if she were afraid of him. One day after dinner with some elderly guests, he and I were leafing through a book of pictures in the *piccola biblioteca* when she joined us through the archway that connected it to the living room. "My two favourite men," she said tipsily, sitting down between us as I moved over.

"Aren't you jumping the gun a little?" Rodolfo asked, coldly closing the book. I recalled hearing a fiery argument as I passed his room on my way to dinner. "Raising Ashley to your brother's level of affection on such brief acquaintance seems a little hasty don't you think?"

"Not in the least." She put her hand on my knee, her emerald eyes sparkling. "I bet Rodolfo hasn't even offered you a drink."

"He hasn't, actually."

"Then let me give you a taste of our local concoction." She went to the drinks table and came back with a colourfully labelled bottle. After offering some to her brother, who declined with a shake of his head, she filled a couple of glasses. "This is called Strega," she said, giving me one of them and sitting down again with her thigh touching mine. "D'you know its origins?"

"No. Should I?"

At this point Rodolfo got up and headed for the drawing room. "*Non m'interessano le tue storie,*" he said coldly.

I glanced at Valeria. An odd look had appeared in her eyes, a mixture of alarm and a sort of indefinable regret. (Is it hindsight speaking? I don't think so, for it struck me even then.) In an instant it was gone. "He says he's not interested in my stories," she translated unnecessarily. "But I think you will be." She raised her glass, peered at the yellow liquid and took a sip. "Have you heard of the witches of Benevento?"

"Vaguely."

"Legend has it that in the Middle Ages young women from these parts would copulate with the devil at midnight. Hence the name of this liqueur, Strega, which means Witch." She picked up the bottle and handed it to me. "That's the founder," she said, pointing at the name Giuseppe Alberti. "The recipe is said to be based on a potion designed to drive out the Barbarigo curse."

"What's the Barbarigo curse?"

She paused as if collecting her thoughts. "Let's say that Giovanni's fling with Caravaggio wasn't the only … improper liaison in our family. In time it became a habit, hence the creation of this drink. Drinking it with a 'legitimate' love object was supposed to exorcise our deviant urges." Suddenly she turned to me, raised her glass and said, "Shall we?" before downing hers while I followed suit. For a while we sat there, she with an impish smile, I basking in my new-found status as her legitimate love object. At last she suggested we go and see the full moon.

At the bottom of a deeply dented stairway we stepped into the balmy night and crossed the courtyard to alight under a colonnade reserved for big dinners in summer. For many minutes we gazed over the forest, barely visible in the dark, to the steady drone of the crickets. From time to time a bat would come fluttering over before swerving away when it sensed us. At last we kissed, clumsily, sexily, as if driven by a delicious inevitability; and then we did it again, more deftly this time, more lingeringly too, while the stars twinkled their approval…

After a while Valeria took me by the hand and led me to the second floor, where I followed her into the Caravaggio room, which I'd heard of but never seen. "Hold your ear in that recess," she said, pointing to one of the corners before stepping out and shutting the door behind her. After a moment I heard her whisper "Do you love me, Ashley?" as unmistakeably as if she were standing by my side. "I do," I breathed. "I love you too," she answered breathily, stirring me to a surge of adoration all the more intense for its lovely circumstance.

When she came back and I asked her to explain the phenomenon she said the second floor had once served as a huge banqueting hall before being turned into four bedrooms linked by the space's original vaults. If spoken into the base of one of the latter, the human voice travelled to its other end with perfect clarity. How on earth could it penetrate the wall between the rooms? I asked, at which she pointed to a small hole in a corner of the ceiling and said, "Through there." Captivated, I asked if there was a name for it, to which she said yes, it was called a whispering gallery. Then we kissed again, this time with the passion of unguarded adoration, before taking our clothes off and making love for the first time. When we were done, I lay there to Valeria's steady breathing, her sweet teenage breathing by my side. As I fell asleep I saw the moon creep into the window frame.

At our marriage three weeks later I wondered whether her eagerness to get it over and done with derived from the fear I might change my mind. Given its short notice, it was a family-only affair. Before the ceremony I lingered outside the local church of Sant' Agnello di Giordano. Though cooler now, the air still held a vestige of summer. Below me lay the forest, all yellows and oranges and reds. After a while I went inside to await Valeria at the altar. Silence reigned; incense filled the air; sunlight lent the nave and walls the colours of the stained-glass windows.

At last, preceded by the cortège – my mother with an old uncle, my father with the contessa and so on – she came in on the arm of the ill-looking count. Rodolfo was absent, busy with his job in Milan, and as they swayed down the aisle to a rickety version of Mendelssohn's Wedding March, my heart swelled with pride at the beauty of my bride. After our honeymoon in Venice, where we stayed at the family Palazzo, the Barbarigo-Montin, we came back to Giordano so that Valeria might see her gynaecologist. When she found out she was pregnant we decided to stay put until the birth. I remember my relief at being able to continue my research on Caravaggio.

## IV

London: the mail drops in through my letterbox; I go to pick it up in the hall: a gas bill, a trade invitation, advertisements and a big A4 envelope. Back at the kitchen table, I open it and bring out a journal called *Art and*

*Aesthetics.* "See leading article p. 4," says a post-it note from my agent. I flip to it. "An Historic Find," says the headline.

For centuries the rumours of Caravaggio's stay at the Castello di Giordano have been brushed off as an old wives' tale. No longer. Last month's publication of Cardinal Giovanni Barbarigo's *Pensieri di un ecclesiastico* has dispelled all doubt. Written between 1587 and 1613 and damaged by fire, we owe its discovery to novice art-historian Ashley Andrews, who submitted it to the only person capable of deciphering its Gothic code, Professor Karl Beck of Tübingen University. The result is astonishing. "This evening," wrote the cardinal on the 2nd of January 1603,

> Michelangelo da Caravaggio arrived at the castle. I have put him up in one of the new bedrooms on the second floor, where he will stay until things have calmed down.

Two weeks later (January the 16th):

> At dinner Caravaggio and I were interrupted by loud banging on the door. A group of armed men had come to arrest him, so I strode to the entrance and said he wasn't here and refused to let them in. In the end my guards came galloping up and drove them away. Seeing Aldobrandini [Ed: Pope Clement VIII] to be on his trail, I have sent him to Altopiano. [Ed: the cardinal's hunting lodge in the hills.]

And finally, a year and a half later (June the 4ᵗʰ 1604):

> On May the 3ʳᵈ Caravaggio was accused in a Roman inn of practising sodomy with me. Angry, he challenged his accuser to a fight. Next day they met at a pallacorda court in the Campo Marzio area (where Caravaggio lives). In the ensuing combat he killed his rival and fled to Naples. What a story!

> For centuries, scholars have debated the cause of the brawl that led to Caravaggio's exile to Naples and Malta. Now at last we have a contemporary explanation. To paraphrase Winston Churchill: never in the field of human learning has history been made in so few words.

I put down the article. It's nothing new, just another in a series of similar pieces; besides, I have more pressing concerns. The child, Ava, was born prematurely but in good health. "Syndactyly is both harmless and operable," said the gynaecologist, spreading out the little girl's webbed fingers. "Still, we must keep an eye out for any further problems." As I sit here I feel a sudden sense of urgency. I pick up his card and dial his number at the Maternità di Benevento. When he answers I identify myself and get straight to the point. Was the child really premature? I ask, my heartbeat threatening my rib cage. A pause follows. "*Sì o no?*" I insist. "I deserve an answer! *Merito una—*"

"*NO!*" he yells. "*Al contrario, era tardiva!*"

"Overdue?" I cry, shocked to hear my hunch validated. A short hush follows. "When was it conceived?"

"A month and a half before the wedding."

I hang up, too upset to say goodbye. A month and a half before the wedding, Valeria and I hadn't even met! And then, suddenly, it all falls into place. The contessa's horror of abortion; Rodolfo's zeal to befriend me; his mother's letter asking him to find someone suitable; finally, his offer to let me investigate the Caravaggio myth. *They needed a father for the child and found him in me!* As I sit there something drops through the letterbox. Surprised, for the mail has already arrived, I get up to fetch it: it is a letter dated yesterday and sent by express courier from Italy. I slip it open. "Adorato," I read.

I can stand it no longer. The thought of your pain grips my heart like a claw. I love you and implore you to come back to me. When I'm with my brother I feel like a rabbit hypnotised by a cobra. Do you recall the night you and I declared our love through the whispering gallery? We'd just drunk Strega together, so I thought I had neutralised the Barbarigo curse. And so I had, at least till Rodolfo's return. His absence from our wedding had nothing to do with his career but to Mamma having thrown him out of the house. Now that Papà is approaching the end, he has come back to prepare for his inheritance.

I look up. Though I was surprised when Rodolfo missed our wedding, it didn't cause me any great concern. On the contrary, I was glad to be rid of him. Even when he came back to say goodbye to his now bedridden father, even then it caused me no more than a vague disquiet till I caught him *in flagrante* with Valeria. Now I wonder at my naïveté, it's all so obvious: his anger as I picked up

Valeria's photograph; his surliness when she and I were together; her anxiety when he was around. I go back to the letter.

> Rodolfo hates little Ava. He thinks her webbed fingers will expose her paternity. I fear he will do her harm. Only you can pry her from his clutches. Only you can save her. I await you urgently, longingly and above all DESPERATELY!
> Come NOW. Don't wait until tomorrow. Come TODAY!!
> Your loving wife,
> Valeria

I put down the note. I am calm now; my mind is made up. Valeria must be rescued from her brother's perversion. I pick up the phone and reserve a seat on the next flight to Benevento. It leaves in three-and-a-half hours and arrives at 18.10. I call a minicab and go upstairs to pack some necessities. Finally I pocket my passport, return to the kitchen and reread Valeria's letter. The doorbell rings; it's the cab; I pocket the note and step bag-in-hand into the street. I reach Gatwick in an hour and a half, in good time for my flight. When I get to the castle I will gather the family into the *salone* (minus the count, who is bed-ridden). Then I will read them Valeria's letter and throw Rodolfo out. If he refuses I shall fetch one of the count's hunting rifles and take the law into my own hands.

# Mea Culpa

## I

Oh, Giselle! If only you could have seen me in my Vatican finery: tails, white bow tie, double-breasted waistcoat and a gold-threaded collar emblazoned with the keys of St Peter. How proud you would have been of me, ushering kings and queens and presidents through pontifical halls into the Holy Father's presence. It might even have garnered me your forgiveness. Today my only hope of redemption is to bare my soul – hence this confession, Giselle, this admission of guilt, this spilling of the beans.

A quarter-century has passed since my induction into the Order of Saint Boniface. As you— I'm sorry, Giselle? I never told you about the Order of Saint Boniface? Then let me enlighten you: founded by my family at the time of the Crusades, it is a charitable organisation aimed at healing the sick and sheltering the poor. Its Grand Master, Cardinal Trifone Tartaruga, was Chairman of Vatican Bank before being retired, in the coy phrase, under a cloud. Today our affiliation rests on a simple quid pro quo: in return for giving them half my fortune (drawn down twice a year so as to keep them keen) I have been granted lifelong refuge in the Order's extraterritorial walls.

This was especially helpful at the beginning. Despite Interpol's repeated calls for my arrest, the Grand Master remained steadfast, insisting that no crime had been discovered in my past; that sharing a killer's name does not a killer make; and that a member of the Order's founding family is *ipso facto* above suspicion. Only in the matter of our little daughter Xenia did he fail me: after many years of searching for her high and low, he gave up the chase. Such is the way of— Where I am? At the high altar of San Mercuzio, site of our family crypt and of Caravaggio's *Siege of Piccarda*, our patron saint's most heroic exploit. What you don't know is that San Mercuzio saw the most terrible trauma of my life, so let me describe it before I get into my unbosoming. I was ten years old and serving as altar boy to Good Friday Mass. The crucifixes were shrouded in lavender velvet and the priest wore his Lenten vestments. At my feet, or rather at my knees, a wooden clapper lay ready to be rattled at the Consecration.

As a non-Catholic you probably don't know what I'm talking about, Giselle, so let me explain. During the three days starting Maundy Thursday, when we Christians honour the Passion of Our Lord, the *crotalus*, as it is called, replaces the traditional consecration bell, which is stored away in the sacristy till Easter Sunday Mass. This time, however, whether through my fault or not, it had been left in its place, and as the celebrant raised the host to Almighty God, I picked it up and gave it the triple-ring that befits every season of the year except the Easter Vigil. Then I put it down again – and froze.

With the best will in the world I could never describe the shiver that ran down my spine as the happy tinkles echoed through San Mercuzio's hallowed walls. It was as if I had disparaged the Passion of Christ, mocked His crucifixion, rejected His divinity itself. As for the priest, unable to disrupt the climax of the Mass, he bent down to kiss the altar before genuflecting in his solemn way and slowly turning around, pallid with outrage. Ponderously he raised his arm and pointed his finger down the aisle like God Almighty casting Adam from the Garden of Eden. A moment later I'd stumbled out to the gaze of five-hundred pairs of eyes including every member of my extended family.

Today, middle-aged as I am, I can appreciate the good padre's reaction. As you know, for I never made any bones about it, I see atonement as the mainstay of my faith and impunity as its anathema – hence my decision to leave Vatican City for the first time in twenty-five years. I have lain low long enough, lived in silks and satins with no hint of expiation for my sin. As from now the good times are over, and so they should be. My destination is the backdrop to our married life; my port of call our fleeting home, the Hôtel de France; my aim to lay bare my misdeeds in all their horror. After over two decades of being kept in the dark by the husband who survived you, you deserve to know the truth.

## II

"*Voilà, monsieur.*"

Good old Roberto's! The same chunks of Parmesan and red leather menus; the same Italian delicacies, unchanged after all these years. When I stepped in, the most I dared hope for were the crisp white tablecloths; or the confectionaries laid out at the entrance (remember the Tarte Tatin with vanilla ice cream or *crème double de Gruyère*?); or the Impressionists adorning the walls – anything to remind me of old times. And what do I find? The whole damn thing just as it was, right down to the cutlery and appetisers, as if the place had been defying the march of time in expectation of my return.

It was dark when I landed last night. After checking in at the hotel – our lover's nest, Giselle, which I made sure to reserve in advance – I took a stroll around my old haunts. Though I expected them to be ruined beyond recall, razed and replaced by a parking lot, I was wrong. A few things *have* changed, of course, not least the Escalier de Gravelle, the old wooden stairway under my student lodgings now exchanged for an ugly concrete ramp. But the rest is exactly as it was, including the little square underneath, with its cobbles and arched colonnade and of course Black's, the object of my ramble.

I first heard about Black's after one of your brother's lunches, his *jeudis chez Jean-Jacques*, as he called them. One of our classmates had brought the host's ex-girlfriend, the willowy Eden, and as I ogled her from a corner of the room – her curves seemed to say "try me and taste heaven" – I wondered at your brother's detachment. Later, on our way to university, I asked him how he could let go of his sweethearts so casually. (I spoke in the plural for it wasn't the first time.) Because they weren't his sweethearts, he answered. Then what were they, I pressed, at which he turned to me and said, "They're chicks from Black's" as if I knew what that meant. When I asked what Black's was, he described it as like a London club with a twist. At first I missed his point, but when at last the penny dropped, I said, "I thought procurement was illegal in this country."

"There's no procurement at Black's," he answered.

"Aren't the girls … paid for services rendered?"

"They're paid to stay at the club until a certain hour," he said. "What they do afterwards is their own business."

That was the beauty of Black's: no pimpery, no obligation, just an extravagant membership fee and a roomful of sweetness. Not a roomful, actually, that would have been too obvious, just a sprinkle, fifteen or twenty, hand-picked to look pretty until closing time. The décor matched the clientèle – indeed, with its crystal glasses and velvet sofas and gentlemen of leisure greeting each other like old friends, it might have been a private home.

Truth to tell, I felt a little nervous when I rang Black's doorbell last night. After all, though I'd paid my fee like clockwork and announced my arrival in advance, I hadn't been back for twenty-five years. Luckily my concern proved vain: after checking my name in his records, the doorman bade me a smiling "*Bienvenu*," so I stepped through the curtain that separates the entrance from the club proper and sat down in a dark corner. Presently a waiter asked what I wanted to drink and I ordered a glass of Heidsieck champagne for old times' sake. Again, nothing had changed: the mirrored bar, the candle-lit tables, the old-master pictures and the restaurant upstairs, all was as it should be – and the girls, of course, each prettier than the last.

Founded in the mid-'60s by a French count and a Greek shipper, Black's has been going strong ever since. Submissions are processed in two steps. After a few months in the candidates' book for the necessary signatures, an applicant is scrutinised by the committee. Blackballing is rare – most entrants withdraw at any whiff of danger – and membership select. There's a strict admission quota

(I forget the number, a couple of hundred, I believe), of which no more than thirty-five are let in at a time. Acceptance is subject to a down-payment so steep that without Jean-Jacques I'd never have been—

"*Avez-vous choisi, monsieur?*"

"*Ah, pardon.*" Poor man! Here I am, lost in reminiscence, while he hovers beside me awaiting my order. (I was tempted to say "*Comme d'habitude*" before realising that it wouldn't even raise a smile, let alone the old knowing nod.) "*Le pot-au-feu, s'il vous plaît.*"

"*Et à boire?*"

"*Avez-vous un Château Haut Brion '79?*"

"*Bien sûr, monsieur. À cinq cent cinquante francs.*"

"*C'est parfait.*"

You know me, Giselle: nothing but the best. Anyway, back to last night. After a moment I spotted a silver-haired man observing me from one of the tables, and though he wouldn't have deserved a second look, his girl was another matter. Lithe of figure, shapely of outline and flawless of face, I suddenly realised who she reminded me of: you, Giselle, you in your prime. Eventually she got up and headed for the exit, and as she made to step through the curtain, she turned around and gave me a smile that fairly melted my heart. And then, as I sat there in perfect happiness, who should shimmer over from the penumbra but the man she had been sitting with. At this point two things fell into place: one, that it was your brother Jean-Jacques, unchanged but for his snow-white mane; and two, that for some reason – my stoop, perhaps, or my crew cut and snowy beard, so different from the long black curls of old, or the paunch that I've been unable to keep in check – he hadn't recognised me. Needless to say I didn't—

"*Voilà, monsieur. Château Haut-Brion 1979.*"

"*Merci.*" Face it, Giselle, there's nothing like a vintage claret, especially a Graves from Pessac-Léo— What's that? How I knew I hadn't been recognised? By his first words. "It's a pleasure to welcome a new member," he said, which was ironic since it was he who'd got me elected in the first place! After a moment I steered the conversation to his girlfriend. She was a club regular, it turned out, and when I asked if she was his lover he said no, just a friend. Instantly I decided to go back the next day, tonight, in other words. Back at the hotel I remembered the—

"*Et votre pot-au-feu.*"

"*Ah, merci.*"

"*Et voici les sauces … gribiche, ravigote, moutarde de Dijon, sauce verte.*"

"*Merci beaucoup.*"

Mmm, just like old times. So where was I? Ah yes, on my way back to the hotel I recalled the beginning of my friendship with your brother. At the end of our first half-term, he asked me to find him a rare book for his collection, a volume of ancient herbs and their medicinal properties to be found only at a specialised shop in Rome. When I gave him the item he asked how much it cost, at which I tripled the amount, declined his refund and awaited my payback. Within days, sure as bacon comes from pigs, he offered to put me up at Black's. We both knew I could never have afforded its membership fee or the prices of its victuals and drink, just as we knew who'd be footing the bill.

On the day I got my letter of acceptance I thanked him

in the hall of the law faculty. "Don't mention it, Leo," he said. "Not only is my money an accident of birth, but I go to places you can't afford. If I didn't do my bit, we'd never be able to hang out together." I remember being touched by his friendship and generosity; I even asked him to join me on my maiden night, but he declined. "Best get your bearings on your own," he said, mindful as ever.

That night I descended the Escalier de Gravelle, crossed the little square, with its stone façades and wooden balconies, and rang Black's doorbell for the first time. (Funny how it comes back to me after so long.) I won't lie to you Giselle: as I slipped through the curtain after checking in my coat, I thought I must have died and gone to heaven. From lithe to curvaceous, from blonde to chestnut, from tall to petite, there was something for everyone. All of a sudden a familiar figure detached itself from the others – Eden, Jean-Jacques's ex, whom I'd met at his place. "Leo," she trilled, turning to me when I called her name, almost as if she were expecting me. "Why don't you sit down and I'll join you in a minute." By the time she came back I'd ordered a bottle of champagne. Ah, Giselle, however much I'd like to do justice to the most electrifying night of my life, I couldn't—

"*Encore un peu?*"

"*Oui, merci. C'est excellent. Transmettez mes félicitations au chef.*"

"*Merci, monsieur.*"

Second helpings are the hallmark of a good restaurant, don't you think, Giselle? God but this is good, as tasty as any— What's that? I should stick to the point? I'm sorry, I keep getting led astray. Where was I? Ah yes, my maiden night at Black's. So there we were, Eden and I, getting to know each other when she suddenly asked to be excused. Without explanation she got up, crossed the room and vanished through a door at one end of the bar only to reappear within an instant – literally so – from an aperture in the wall beside me, like a magic trick. To my delight she'd changed into a light chiffon frock that left little to the imagination. A moment later she flitted out again before re-emerging through yet another door, this time in an outfit showing endless legs, a bare midriff and a cleavage giving riotous food for thought. By now my blood felt like mulled wine spiked with adrenaline, but though I assumed her to be playing a trick on me, I missed the point until her third or fourth appearance. This time she sat down beside me in a see-through minidress that had my eyes fairly popping out of their sockets and my hands itching to cop a feel.

And then, suddenly, as I sat there trying to control myself, she looked over my shoulder at someone behind me. So I turned around – and gasped! Observing us with an artful little smile stood a clone of Eden's: the same curves, the same face, the same hairdo, the same everything. Nirvana, she was called, Eden's identical twin, nineteen years old to my twenty-one. After getting over my shock I ordered another bottle of champagne, which we guzzled down amid naughty conversation, and then a third. Eventually I followed them, pleasantly tipsy, to their flat for a night of lust such as I had never known. So good was Black's champagne – Heidsieck '62, of course, the world's most delicious drink – that its effect on our frolics proved the opposite of what I might have feared.

For several weeks I went back for more, intermittently at first and then every night, and the process was always the same. Now and then I might rope in Nirvana or one of the other girls, but it was Eden who became the focus of my desire. You know how it is with a sexual infatuation, it's like a mania, an *idée fixe*, and by the time of the events described below, I'd got her firmly under my—

"*Vous avez fini, monsieur?*"

"*Oui, merci.*"

"*Un dessert?*"

"*Pourquoi pas. Le zabaglione s'il vous plaît.*"

Oddly enough, it was the day after my first night at Black's that you and I met at one of Jean-Jacques's lunches. For some reason it was just the three of us, you, me and him, and with the *omertà* by which the club was treated in female company, not a word was breathed about my doings of the night before. (Later, of course, I briefed him in every detail.) When the talk turned to your parents' death in a private plane crash, I found out that you'd inherited the chalet in the mountains and your brother the house in Mustique with the cash split fifty-fifty between you – none of which fell on deaf ears, as you can imagine.

A fortnight later Jean-Jacques left for his Caribbean Christmas, giving me carte blanche to strut my stuff at Black's. At first I held back, less for any false politesse or discretion than for my own year-end holiday in the mountains. Eager to get to know you, I'd taken a room in a nearby village – anything else would have been unaffordable – from which I inveigled myself into the *clique de Giselle*, as your circle was known. A day on the slopes would take us to Charlie's Tea Room for a nut cake or a chestnut purée with double cream, before heading home to change for dinner at the Olden Restaurant or the Palace Hotel followed by dancing and drinking and snorting coke at the recently opened GreenGo nightclub – all at your generous expense.

But after a while the pull of Black's proved stronger than me. Late in the morning of New Year's Day I cancelled our tête-à-tête dinner, much to your disappointment, and drove back home. You know about the mice when the cat's away, don't you? Well never was it more feverishly confirmed. Night after night I would order my Heidsieck or a '61 Dom Pérignon at six-hundred francs a bottle and share it with whomever was around. From time to time I might consider something cheaper, Stolichnaya, say, or a single-malt Scotch or even a prosecco, before recoiling from the shame of losing face before the girls. Slap-up dinners followed on the first floor, chefs-d'oeuvre of French gastronomy washed down with the choicest clarets and rounds of Rémy Martin.

When Jean-Jacques came back from Mustique he was met by a ten-thousand-franc bill from Black's, a huge sum in those days, enough for a big car. Truth to tell I was surprised at his reaction: I hadn't thought him capable of anger but I was wrong, as I soon— I'm sorry Giselle? I might have expected it? That's easy for you to say. Hadn't he vowed to do his bit so we could go out together? A crook, he called me, a schemer and a scrounger; he even accused me of fraud, which hurt. At first I thought it would blow over, but a couple of days later he intercepted me in the big lecture hall and said, "I met with my lawyer yesterday."

"Your lawyer?" I parroted, smelling a rat.

"Yes, he's going to send you a letter."

"Saying what?"

"That either I get my money back or I take you to court."

My reaction dwells with me. A moment of panic led to a sort of epiphany, a prying open of my future. Skipping the day's classes I went home, packed a few necessities and drove straight to your chalet in Gstaad. When you opened the door, I said I needed to see you, could I come in? Of course, you answered, as I knew you would, your eyes sparkling with surprise and adoration. At the sight of my suitcase you invited me to spend the night.

Over a fireside fondue, I laid out the pretext for my visit: that I couldn't get you out of my mind; that I'd sown my wild oats and needed to settle down; and that you were the only girl I wished to share my life with. After taking your virginity I popped the question (in your annoying phrase). Remember our wedding? The tiny wooden chapel; the snow-covered fir trees; Jean-Jacques's refusal to attend? Even when I reimbursed him (with your money, of course) he stayed up on his high horse, even skipping Xenia's baptism at the Église St-Joseph. How sweet were her squeals as the holy water trickled over her little forehead. Later we invited my childless aunt Antoinette, the baby's godmother, for lunch at your parents' former suite in the Hôtel de France. And so things—

"*Un café, monsieur?*"

"*Pourquoi pas. Un espresso s'il vous plaît.*"

And so things might have stood but for an unexpected twist of fate about nine months later. You'd driven up to Gstaad to prepare the chalet for the season; as usual when

I was by myself, I went to Roberto's for lunch. By then my mind had been turning to Eden more and more often, and as I sat there awaiting my apéritif I imagined her floating through the door in her ethereal way. And then, in one of those singular moments when destiny steps in to grant one's unspoken wishes, in she strolled on Jean-Jacques's arm.

By now your brother would have nothing to do with me, so he steered Eden to a table in the far corner of the room. Knowing his routine like the inside of my pocket – how often had he bought me lunch here – I sat back and bided my time. As usual he placed his order and asked for a glass of sherry before going downstairs to wash his hands. No sooner was he out of sight than I crossed the room and handed Eden the number of the Hôtel de France with the words "Call me before 3.30." Then I retraced my steps basking in the satisfaction of a scheme well planned. A moment later Jean-Jacques came back, blissfully unaware of the plot that had unfolded in his absence.

When she rang, as I knew she would, I suggested tea for old times' sake. *Pourquoi pas*, she replied, knowing exactly what she was about, and within half an hour I'd met her in the lobby and led her to the room I'd taken for the occasion. I shan't lie to you, Giselle, the next hour-and-a-half was the most erotic of my life, with Eden surpassing the Kamasutra as only she knew how. How I'd missed her, I thought as we lay there in post-coital languor: the smooth skin; the dark-brown hair; the twitch of her nose when she spoke; and the curves, lissom and slim apart from where it mattered. And then we did it again, less frenziedly, more languorously, more dreamily too…

Later I was reaching for my cigarettes as I always do after making love, when the sight of my watch on the bedside table gave me the shock of my life. Five-fifteen, it said, a quarter of an hour before your expected return! Frantically we threw on our clothes and hastened downstairs, where I saw Eden out through the hotel's revolving door. Then I turned around, pleased as punch – and gasped! There you sat, Giselle, the wronged wife, studying me from a corner of the foyer. (You'd been tipped off by the concierge, as I found out later, which came as no surprise, they never liked me, they called me Monsieur Giselle.)

Even then we might have saved the day if you'd been a little more trusting. Not only did I mean it when I promised never to see Eden again, but I kept my word. The girl you "caught me with," as you put it, two weeks later, wasn't Eden at all but her twin sister, who'd married a client of Black's and come back from her honeymoon. After bumping into each other in the lounge we chatted for a while and parted ways. That was all, I swear, as I did then, over and over, but you wouldn't listen, you called it the most pathetic lie you'd ever heard. (With hindsight it must have sounded pretty far-fetched, but it was true, I swear on what honour I have left that it was true.) What did it in the end, what tore my patience once and for all, was your vow to cut me off from your bank account when the Crédit Suisse opened in the morning.

As you can imagine I slept badly that night; I was too busy concocting my plan. First thing next day I rang Cardinal Tartaruga, Grand Master of the Order of Saint Boniface, to give him the lie of the land and negotiate his pound of flesh. Then I went to the bank and transferred all your money, which I still had full access to, into my account, complete with a monthly payment to the Order (not forgetting the cardinal's commission). Finally I boarded your jet – our jet, as I still thought of it, albeit for the last time – late that morning. Two hours later, while your body had yet to be found, I was waved through customs and whisked off to Vatican City. Within a week I'd become the twentieth member of my family to become a Knight of Saint Boniface by Papal Command. Finally – finally! – I had made up for my childhood misdeed, and as I stepped out of the induction room with the Silver Rabbit round my neck, I felt as if the weight of the world had fallen off my shoulders. Ever since—

"*Votre addition, monsieur.*"

Ah, the bill.

## III

What's that, Giselle?— why I keep staring at that graffito? Because unlike the others, which are shrouded in darkness, it's lit by the streetlamp outside. In case you can't make it out it depicts a nymph with her hand down her knickers captioned RISK in capital letters. The guy next door spent half the night yelling out drunken babble until the rattle of his cell door led to a dull thump followed by silence. Me, I was different: never resist arrest, they say, and seldom was the adage more apt. So let me resume.

After yesterday's lunch at Roberto's I went to the bank for my planned wire transfer, which took a while given its size. Back at the— I'm sorry? What transfer? All in good time, Giselle, all in good time. Back at the hotel I took a nap followed by a bath and room service. At eleven I went to Black's and sat down to await the girl from the night before, which didn't take long. Within barely a minute she came levitating towards me almost as if we had a date. Adorable she was, all cherry lips and ready smiles.

And then, suddenly, who should saunter over but your brother. "Have you been introduced?" he asked, unctuously sitting down between us. "We haven't, actually," she replied. "In that case, allow me," he said, spreading his hands. "Leo, this is Xenia; Xenia, this is your papa." Then he turned to the entrance and raised his arm, causing a plain-clothes policeman to cross the room and put his hand on my shoulder. "You are under arrest for the murder of your wife Giselle on December 15th 1972," he said. A minute later I was handcuffed and on my way to prison.

What's that? If I was caught off-guard? Come come, Giselle, you know me better than that. Remember the baby's godmother, my aunt Antoinette who married Edmond de Sorailles, the richest man in France? When she died childless I inherited her fortune. That was two months ago, and ever since, two conflicting words have buzzed before my mind's eye like a pair of busy bees: atonement and impunity, atonement and impunity, atonement and impunity. Gradually a plan of action took shape in my head. First I would quit my extraterritorial home; second I would make amends at the scene of my crime; and third I would— What's that? I'm lying? Don't be ridiculous, Giselle! Why else would I have put my head in the lion's mouth? Or warned Black's of my arrival in the knowledge that it would reach your avengers? D'you really think I didn't know that I'd been recognised, that my fate—

I'm sorry? Why I didn't give myself up instead of planning this silly rigmarole? Because I *wanted* Jean-Jacques to vindicate his sister and little Xenia her mother. Oh, I know what you think: that I'm beyond shame, incapable of remorse, which may be true but it's beside the point. The point is retribution, hence my decision to wire Xenia her godmother's bequest. From one day to the next our daughter has become a wealthy woman. Now I can sit back in the satisfaction of having made up for my crime, wiped the slate clean from the prison cell that will lodge me for the rest of my life. Do you remember the Book of Genesis, Giselle? "On the seventh day God saw what he had made, and behold, it was good." Well so it goes with me. I see what I have made, and behold, it is good.

# The Past is Never Dead,
# it is not Even Past

"Noia," screams the placard outside the station. "The World's Oldest University." They can't seem to shake off the old canard, can they? As everyone knows, Bologna leads the pack before Oxford and Cambridge and Noia doesn't even figure in the top ten. Yet they keep on flogging the dead hoax. Instead of encouraging mass tourism like its peers, Noia has kept a lid on its past, refusing to tout its landmarks or quirky street names. The main square is called Piazza della Presa in Giro (Mockery Square); the food market, Foro delle Palle Rotte (Forum of the Broken Balls); and the shopping street Via della Porca Miseria (Goddamnit Street) – though the funniest of all must be the Corso Fittizio (Fictional Boulevard)! Each rests on some bizarre mediaeval legend, and if more were made of them I might not have alighted in a ghost town. It's as if— Ah, there's a cab. "TAXI, TAXI!"

Founded by Charles the Fat, Noia was named after his father's last words, *Che noia*, meaning what a bore. That much is known, unlike the canard about the founding of the university by Louis the Blind, which is plucked out of the ether. The buildings around the main square are of travertine marble quarried in the local hills and include a small but beautiful *duomo*, a *residenza episcopale* and a *municipio*. Depending on the position of the sun, they change colour like chameleons. Dawn lends them a silvery grey; noon a blinding glare (at least in summer); and sunset a golden glow. As the cab winds through my student stomping grounds I feel a surge of nostalgia.

"*Grazie*," says the driver as I pay him outside 38 Via Senza Nome (Street Without a Name). I recognise the door, I used to pass it on my way to Ginevra's parents' place. I've made a note of the access code on my iPhone, here it is: 39A45. God the door's heavy, and loud too, crashing shut behind me in a racket fit to raise the dead. Third floor, said the email, flat 32, "you'll find the key under the doormat." I love these wrought-iron lifts, they're solid and durable. Far from sighing into life and whisking you to your objective like their flimsy modern counterparts, they lurch out of hibernation and hoist you to your floor amid clangs of protest at being woken up.

How clever is the sharing economy. Like many a brain-wave – with certain exceptions such as the split atom, say, or palaeomagnetism – Airbnb might have been invented by anyone. Getting home-owners to let you rent out their properties in return for a portion of the income, what could be simpler than that? A straightforward idea smoothly put to work and all of a sudden you're a billion-aire. The system varies, but boils down to this: you find a place online, check its pictures and reviews, book it if you like and can afford it and get an email telling you at what time it'll be available, the location of the key and the hour by which you have to leave (usually noon of the last day). No meeting and greeting, no trying to impress anyone, no human contact at all, in fact, just in and out at will.

The landing is nondescript; the silence complete; the

lock a bit stiff but it works. The flat looks just as it did on the website, bland but pleasant. A simple wardrobe; an artificially faded modern kilim; a grey Ikea sofa flanked by two matching armchairs. Let's see if the view's as brilliant as it's touted. Yes, not bad, and how different from the fog of London! There's the Monte Maestro, its summit topped by a little cloud like the belch of a volcano before it erupts. And there's the city park, its features clearly visible; the university and its outbuildings; the pavilion where a tinny band used to play Donizetti or Leoncavallo on public holidays; and the bench that witnessed my first meeting with Ginevra. Though my heart was in my mouth as I approached – for weeks I'd observed her cold-shouldering her male admirers – she smiled and tapped the space next to her as if to say let's chat. Close-up I spotted a little mole above the right corner of her mouth.

The moment summed up our respective personalities: she, casual and relaxed; I, bumbling and insecure. Which didn't stop her from inviting me to her parents' country house the following Sunday. "Bring your swimming gear if the weather's good," she said. (It was and I did.) I still remember Alessandro Colombo, the local Don Juan, buzzing around her like a bee around a honeypot. How ecstatic I felt when she chose me over him! Last week, while toying with the idea of going back to Noia half a century after these events, I wondered if I should look her up – what could be more cathartic than to face the first woman ever to own one's heart? – but in the end I thought better of it. She must be withered and wrinkly and married with a brood of grown-up children: best keep our memories intact.

It took years for me to forget her, but in the end I did. Only the faded picture that jumped out at me while I was tidying up my belongings brought her back to my consciousness. Her smile from that very bench sparked a flood of memories: of her love of fun; of her dusky skin and chestnut hair; of her lack of artifice and seeming unawareness of her effect on men. Only when she wished to sway someone, a professor, say, who had given her a bad mark, or a *vigile urbano* sliding a ticket behind the windscreen wiper of her parents' car, or some vendor on the flea market – only then would she wake up to the quality that defined her.

That's the church bell tolling twelve noon. I used to hear it when I spent the night at Ginevra's parents' place up the street. Mostly they stayed at their country house, but even when they were in town their presence never cramped our frolics. I remember our first time. En route to the family flat she told me they must be watching TV but not to worry, they wouldn't mind or even second-guess what we were up to, so long as we kept quiet. She wore a red miniskirt, and on our way upstairs I caught a flash of her naked bottom (and more). By the time we tiptoed into her room I was panting with lust.

Twelve-ten, I'd better get going, I'm to meet up with Filippo at our former haunt, the Osteria del Studente. I remember when we met. It was our second day and I was scouring the notice board when he made a remark about our syllabus. After that we became fast friends; like Siamese twins we did everything together. Not only was he always good for a laugh but he would help me when I ran out of money at the end of the month. His father was an army general and hero of the Dodecanese Campaign whose regiment included Alessandro Colombo, Ginevra's main admirer, who'd stuck around, much to my annoyance, even after she and I became an item.

One day I asked Filippo to convince his old man to transfer Alessandro to Milan or Genoa or even further north. He would see what he could do, he answered, helpful as ever, though I didn't give it much credence. (Generous as he was, he tended to overpromise and underdeliver.) Ten days later, to my enormous surprise and gratitude, the greatest threat to my relationship with Ginevra was packed off to Bologna. Later, when she dumped me, Filippo acted as our go-between, and if he failed to mend our relationship it wasn't for lack of trying. Every other day he would bring her my latest begging letter before returning with a verbal or written rejection that seemed to hold a glimmer of hope (or so I kidded myself). So I would try again, over and over, until at last I surrendered to the indisputable and left town the day after obtaining my degree.

I think I'll cross the park; it may not be the fastest route but I feel like making a pilgrimage to the bench where I met Ginevra. An old woman moves over when I approach. The university can be glimpsed through the bushes, as old as the hills, like everything in this town. I remember Carlo Levi's take on Eboli: "Bypassed by Christianity, by morality, by history itself, excluded from the full human experience." He might as well have been referring to Noia.

What's the time, 12.25, I'd better get on with it. *"Arrivederci"* – oh, she's left, I didn't see her go. Along the familiar route, nothing has changed: the pavilion; the iron gate to the Piazza Penosa (Painful Square); the Teatro Carlo Goldoni, named after the Venetian playwright; and the tavern supposedly once used by Michelangelo. Whenever I was asked why I chose to study in such a backwater I would put it down to the thrill of attending the world's oldest seat of learning. (In those days I still believed the fib.)

I wonder if they've redone the interior of the university; in my day it had a well-worn stairway lined with busts of Greek and Roman philosophers. The desks were carved with slogans too old to decipher. One morning after our course in International Law, I gestured for Ginevra to come over. When she arrived I pointed out my favourite image: a heart pierced with an arrow over a barely legible caption. She asked what it said and I answered, "*Il mio amore è eterno*," so she leaned over and gave me a kiss. (At the time she still shared my feelings…)

The Osteria del Studente … like everything else, it's hardly changed. Ah, there's Filippo, though I doubt I'd have recognised him if I'd passed him in the street. Even close-up I see little of his former self. Gone is the twinkle in his eye, his roguish style and casual geniality, replaced by the traces of too much food and drink and tobacco. He gets up, slightly stooped, very overweight, like a man who's never begrudged himself the good things in life, and cries, "*Benvenuto!*" He's wearing a grubby cardigan and a pair of old cords. With a pipe in his mouth he'd be a picture-book old codger.

Ah, that's *Marina* on the radio, the big hit of our student days; what nostalgia it causes me, a longing for our many coffees here, often with Ginevra. When I mention it, he nods slowly and says there's nothing like music to bring back the past. We reminisce about old classmates, some dead, some alive, some ill, some healthy, some successful, others not (including the two of us); of our parents, all four of them dead; of our jobs and grown-up children and of Facebook, agent of our reconnection. After a while the waiter asks what we would like. Loath to interrupt our nostalgia, we order arancini with tomato sauce and the house wine. "*Per tre*," Filippo adds.

"For three?" I ask when the man has gone.

"Yes, my wife will be joining us in a minute."

His wife … so complete was our parting that I had no idea he was married. "Where's she from?" I ask.

"Calabria."

"When did you marry?"

"Three weeks after I got my degree." He lights a cigarette with the chrome army lighter I know so well. "She was already three months pregnant."

I frown with puzzlement. "So you were with her during our last term."

"Oh yes," he says quietly, taking a drag and exhaling. "And the one before."

What's that weight in my stomach? I lean back while the waiter fills our glasses. After he has gone, we sit there for a while in silence. Suddenly I hear my voice say, "Do you know why I accepted your invitation to come and see you after so long?"

"Tell me."

"Because I wanted to thank you for trying to save my relationship with Ginevra. You acted like a true friend. That you weren't able—"

"It was nothing."

"That you weren't able to bring us back together wasn't your fault. You did your best."

He shakes his head, looking sombre. "Don't thank me, I didn't—"

"When you got your father to send Alessandro Colombo to Bologna, I thought my love was finally ... in the clear." Slowly I shake my head. "It's pathetic."

"Don't say that."

"Why not?"

He stubs out his half-smoked cigarette. "Because I didn't ... do it for you."

I frown in perplexity; what's he talking about? "Do what for me?"

"Get Alessandro transferred."

I keep my eyes on him. "Then who did you do it for?"

"Myself."

The weight in my stomach just got a little heavier. "I don't understand."

Suddenly he looks towards the door and raises his arm. I turn around; it's the old woman from the park bench. "*Ciao, cara,*" he says as she approaches – and then, turning to me, "I'd like you to meet my wife."

My first impression is of a familiar smile; my second of a little mole above the corner of her mouth; and my third of something intensely toxic coursing through my veins. We sit down and she says "*Come va?*" in the Calabrese accent that once meant so much to me. I don't answer, my mind is too busy veering from disbelief to mortification and from mortification to an odd sense of freedom, as if a load that has been weighing me down since time out of mind has finally been lifted.

All of a sudden two feelings strike me at the same time: first: the wish to be somewhere else, anywhere but there; second, the sense of my legs lifting me up like alien organs untethered to my will. Zombie-like I head for the exit and set off for my Airbnb flat. The weather has changed; a light drizzle fills the air. I pass the theatre, cross the park and climb the slope that leads to the old city. (The cobbler on the Via Disperata has given way to a mini-supermarket.)

From the flat I order an Uber, put my key on the table (as instructed) and pick up my suitcase. The lift is still on my floor, as if it's been awaiting me, so I step in and punch the button marked 0. After moment it reaches the ground floor amid the usual protestations. My car draws up just as I exit the house. The driver reciprocates my greeting and puts my luggage in the boot as I slip onto the back seat. From Reggio I'll take the train to Rome and the next flight to London. Do I regret coming back? The answer hits me on the heels of the question: that I don't; that my aim wasn't to meet an old friend but to banish my demons at the scene of their mischief; and that I got what I wanted and more. On the Viale dell' Esorcismo (Exorcism Avenue) I remember a line by Faulkner. "The past is never dead, it is not even past." Until now I embodied that quip. No longer: for the first time in my life my past has evanesced and I'm free.

# Kristina Ramsis

I

She lingered in the doorway of the hotel restaurant; the sole diner seemed to have finished his meal; waiters hung about with nothing to do; to her right, floor-to-ceiling windows revealed a lit rock garden sloping down to the (invisible) Red Sea. She stepped in and slalomed between the tables towards the young man scrutinising his BlackBerry. When she reached him she apologised for troubling him and asked if his other chair was free. "Free?" he said, looking up as if abruptly brought back to earth.

"Yes; being by ourselves I thought we might as well meet."

"Of course! I'm so sorry!" He got up and pulled it out. "Please."

"You've evidently had dinner," she said, sitting down. A TV was droning in the background.

"I have. But I can keep you company if you like." In his mid-to-late twenties, like her, he exuded a sort of self-confident fragility, if that wasn't a contradiction in terms.

She smiled. "With pleasure." A waiter handed her the menu and stood back while she scanned it. After ordering *ful medames* – beans with eggs and vegetables – she turned to her companion. "Kristina Ramsis," she said, holding out her hand for him to shake.

He did so. "Bishoy Issa."

"Issa ... isn't that Arabic for Jesus?"

"Indeed." He paused without taking his eyes off her. *"Enti betkellem Arabi?"*

"Sadly not. My father left Egypt before I was even thought of, so I'm British born and bred. And my mother's French, which doesn't help."

"What brings you to the land of your forebears in these troubled times?"

"I'm an architect; my company was short-listed for the British University's new campus in Heliopolis; given my family background I was charged with making the presentation."

"And? How did it go?"

"I haven't made it yet. It was scheduled for next Tuesday but it's been postponed due to the political unrest. I found out only yesterday."

He gave a shy smile. "So you came to Egypt for nothing."

She shrugged. "So it seems."

"What are you going to do?"

"My boss says I should get myself out of harm's way. I told him all London flights were cancelled or overbooked."

"Is that true?"

"No, but it could be." She'd felt no qualms about lying to Desmond: her job was a grind, she'd just dumped her boyfriend – another dud – and the weather in London was its usual grey self. "The truth is, I can't bear to go back home yet."

"So what are you going to do?" he repeated.

"I was thinking of flying to Cairo on Tuesday. Maybe the—"

"Are you crazy? All hell's about to break loose."

Suddenly, as if on cue, a news alert caught his attention. She observed him as he sat there, his eyes glued to the TV: full lips, longish curls, dusky skin, slightly curved nose, he might have played the title role in a film about Tutankhamun.

"Unbelievable!" he exclaimed, his eyes on the monitor. "Never before has so massive a political rally converged anywhere in the world. The biggest demonstration ever! Can you imagine?" He shook his head. "History in the making!"

For a while they sat there while the commentator droned on in Arabic. At last her food arrived. "So what's going to happen?" she asked, taking a mouthful and finding it delicious.

"Trouble," he said. "Big trouble; but good trouble, necessary trouble. You can't make an omelette without breaking eggs, as it were." At an image of President Morsi appearing onscreen, he gave a snort of contempt. "Whoever takes that clown's place it'll be good riddance."

"Don't you like Morsi?"

He lit a cigarette with a slight tremor of his hand. "Judging by your name you're a Copt," he said, seemingly avoiding her question.

"That's right," she answered. "And you?"

"Same. No Copt likes Morsi."

"What about the Muslims?"

He hailed one of the waiters. "What's your name?" he asked in English.

"Ali."

"Are you Christian or Muslim, Ali?"

"Muslim, Sir."

"And what do you think of Morsi?"

"Between Morsi and the devil I vote for the devil," the man replied, poker-faced.

"*Shukran, Ali.*" He turned back to her. "See? It's not sectarian, it's across the board."

"How come you speak such good English?" she asked.

"Because my grandmother was Irish, from Galway. We've been bilingual for two generations."

She looked at him. "Why don't you tell me about yourself," she said. "It seems we have time on our hands."

"Indeed." Flicking the ash off his cigarette, he leaned back as if to arrange his thoughts. There was a languor about him, an old-world poise that she found attractive. At the turn of the century his great-grandfather set up a cotton-ginning factory in Beni Mazar, he began. Within a couple of years it had grown into one of the biggest in Egypt. Five decades later his sons sold it so as to avoid Nasser's nationalisation; with the proceeds they bought the Memphis Group of Hotels. "Three years ago they predicted a decline in tourism due to political instability and sold it at the top of the market."

"Amazing!" she cried. "Who made the decision?"

"My father and his brother Boutros."

"They must have been very proud."

"They were, though my father wasn't able to enjoy his windfall for very long. He died of a heart attack eleven months ago. Twenty-one years after my mother."

"So you're an orphan."

He nodded slowly.

"And a wealthy heir."

He sat there while the comment hovered awkwardly

between them. Seeing a shadow settling on his face, she regretted making it. "*Tempi passati...*" he murmured with a shake of his head. At last he turned to her. "Now you."

She gave him the short version. Her father was from Alexandria; aged nineteen he went to study medicine in London, where he married a classmate and stayed put; after a year-and-a-half they had twins, a boy and a girl. At first they'd found it hard to make ends meet, but soon he became a sought-after surgeon. Pausing while the waiter delivered her coffee, she wondered how much to reveal. His infidelities? His abuse of his wife and daughter? Its impact on her love life? She recalled a statement of her mother's: "When the dog's sick you're all over it. As soon as it's well you ignore it. Hence your choice of boyfriends, I suppose: deadbeats to a man." God knew she had a point. Her last lover, an alcoholic writer, was being sued by his publisher for breach of contract.

"You were talking about your father," Bishoy cut in when the waiter had left.

"Yes. When I was fifteen he fell in love with a nurse and moved out of the family home. Since then I haven't seen much of him. At university I gained my degree in architecture before joining the studio of Desmond Burroughs." She smiled. "That's it. Not very interesting, I'm afraid."

He smiled politely. "On the contrary."

Later, at the bar, they drank grappa and chatted away to a disco soundtrack. Just as she was making to call it a day Bishoy turned to her. "I have an idea for tomorrow," he said, stubbing out another cigarette to the sound of *How Deep Is Your Love?* "Let's go to Luxor and see the sights."

"Luxor?" she parroted.

"Yes. The pride of Egypt. Given the political insecurity we'll have it to ourselves. It's a golden opportunity."

## II

The road cut through the sand like an arrow-straight ribbon of grey. To left and right, dunes stretched out into the horizon. Mirages on the tarmac vanished like chimerical puddles as they approached. From time to time a roadblock would force the driver to slow down before getting waved on by a slovenly soldier. But for the Nile Egypt would be a lunar landscape, Kristina thought: ten per cent of the country housed ninety per cent of the population. Gradually, oases gave way to mud villages, springs to little waterways, and at dusk they reached the only river fit to call itself the birthplace of western civilisation.

At the hotel a bellboy picked up their suitcases and led them into the lobby. While Bishoy was checking them into a pair of separate rooms, she picked up a booklet from the reception. "A temple of tradition surrounded by lush gardens and millenarian sights," she read. "Inspired by its old-world ambience, Agatha Christie wrote *The Sphinx is the Riddle* in suite 27." Kristina put it down and scanned the foyer. Under a wrought-iron gallery and a massive Murano chandelier, fez-bedecked bellboys stood idly by. A pair had stepped out to smoke.

In her room she unpacked and turned on her laptop. Her inbox contained an email from her boss, Desmond Burroughs. "You did well to stay put," he wrote. "All other foreign contestants have fled the country and I doubt they'll be back soon. At this rate you'll be able to grab the job by default. So sit tight until the dust settles." She closed the email and opened the front page of *The Times*. Seeing nothing new about Egypt she folded her computer and went to join Bishoy for an early dinner. In the restaurant, plates and silverware were disposed on crisp white tablecloths amid napkins stitched with the emblem of the hotel. Again they were the only diners.

Over coffee Kristina cleared her throat and repressed the hesitation she'd felt all day. "There's something I've been meaning to ask you," she said.

He turned to her. "Please."

"Yesterday, when I asked rather brashly if you were a wealthy heir, you referred to *tempi passati* as if to make a point." She waited for any trace of awkwardness. Seeing none, she completed her train of thought. "Not to be indiscreet, but … what did you mean?"

He leaned back, his eyes half-shut, his air deadpan in the way he had about him. Once more she scanned him for any sign of outrage or offence but found none. "Your question isn't indiscreet at all," he said. "In fact I welcome it." With his usual tremor he lit his third cigarette. "The truth is, I've dragged myself down from heaven on earth to the lowest circle of hell, as it were, entirely through my own fault." For several seconds he stared at the ceiling. "To the best of my belief no one knows the story but its protagonists. It harks back to my time at the American University in Cairo. Though my father would have preferred me to read business studies, he never rammed things down my throat. Despite his regret he supported my choice of comparative literature; soon I was delving into my favourite writers, from Dickens to Flaubert and from Naguib Mahfouz to Omar Khayyam. One of my classmates was a quiet Coptic girl called Hawwa, and gradually we fell in love. My father was thrilled, seeing her single-mindedness as a foil to my lethargy.

"A case in point occurred at the close of our third term. The system required a minimum average mark to ensure one's promotion to the next year. On the big day we congregated around the notice board to check our results, and as I stood there I heard Hawwa curse under her breath. To her disbelief, she'd failed by a single decimal point. Next day she requested a meeting with the professor of her best subject. What kind of system would allow a student's entire year to be scuppered by so razor-thin a margin, she asked with righteous indignation. If he added a decimal point to his mark he'd get her out of the woods, as it were. At first he balked – the rules were the rules, there was nothing for it – but after being cajoled and beleaguered for days on end, he finally gave way. All the while she'd kept her friends in the dark, even me, no doubt to save face if her plan miscarried. It was classic Hawwa, determined yet discreet, which was one of the reasons I fell in love with her.

"At the start of the next term she told her parents that she no longer needed an allowance. Apart from the use of the family home, she wished to stand on her own two feet. To get by she'd taken a job as a freelance guide in the Egyptian Museum. One day at the Café Riche, the old restaurant on Talaat Harb a few minutes from the university, we were joined by a very pretty friend of hers called Nazli with her fiancé, a cool young man called Mahmoud Mubarak. In the weeks to come I kept bumping into them: you know how it is, you meet someone for the first time and they pop up at every turn. One night I bumped into Nazli at a disco called the Piranha in the Būlāq district. Being by myself – Hawwa was at home finishing an essay – I bought her a drink and then another, and gradually our banter grew flirtatious. In the end I took her home. She was a sexy little thing, and after a year of unveering monogamy, I couldn't resist.

"Next morning I woke up unusually late, so I brewed us some coffee and saw Nazli off before getting dressed and rushing to university. After lunch with Hawwa at the Café Riche I escorted her to the Egyptian Museum as I often did. While crossing Tahrir Square, with its demented traffic and traces of political unrest, she shouted, 'I left my Bongioanni behind this morning.' 'What – *again?*' I countered with a laugh. (Forgetting her guidebook was an inveterate habit of hers and a standing joke between us.) 'Yes, again!' she chuckled. 'On my way to university I had to go back and fetch it'."

At this point in Bishoy's story Kristina put her hand on his arm. "I'm sorry to interrupt," she said. "But the waiters are getting edgy. I think they want us to go."

At the bar Bishoy ordered two grappas before lighting yet another cigarette, his fourth, as far as she could tell. He seemed to have something on his mind. At last he said there was an aspect of the story he'd left out. "The events I just described go back barely a month," he said laconically.

"Really!" she exclaimed, genuinely surprised. "They sounded like ancient history."

He nodded slowly. "Probably because of their ill-omened mood." When their drinks came, he downed his and asked for another. "No doubt you remember that my father died a year ago. As an only child and an orphan I got his entire estate, including our duplex apartment over the Nile. Though I didn't realise it until later, it proved more of a curse than a blessing, like a time bomb, as it were." After another pause he shook his head. "Anyway, after my night with Nazli, Hawwa and I went back to our old routine: lectures at university, lunches at the Café Riche, dinners at home and the odd night out. Meanwhile I sensed our bond tightening, perhaps from guilt on my part, and gradually I made the decision to ask for her hand in marriage.

"One day I hosted a dinner at my place, and though we lived apart – anything else would have been highly improper – she acted as my hostess, as she always did on such occasions. At the sight of her playing house so sweetly, I vowed to take the plunge before the week was out. At about midnight someone suggested the Piranha, and despite a pang of discomfiture, I joined the group. We found it packed with friends, not least Mahmoud, Nazli's fiancé, though without his other half, as it were. When Hawwa left – she had a job first thing in the morning – I stayed on, and in the small hours he invited me to his apartment for a nightcap. After pouring me a drink he suggested a game of backgammon."

In the pause that followed, Bishoy lit another cigarette before slowly putting his matches back in his pocket. Everything was ponderous about him, even the most mundane task. On a TV above the bar, a political talk-show was getting heated, but he didn't seem to care or even notice. Slowly, almost wearily, he began to describe

his game of backgammon. She'd seen it before: the profes-
sional granting the amateur a few victories so as to rouse
his greed; the setbacks cleverly interspersed to fire up his
resolve; the odd bone casually thrown in to raise the stakes.
It was the classic gamblers' *pas de deux*: experience leading
doggedness to ruin. Suddenly he leaned forward, put out
his half-smoked cigarette and said he had to go to the
bathroom. Alone now, Kristina sat back, amazed at what
she'd been hearing. All of a sudden her old lovers struck
her as mere heralds of this Shakespearean calamity…

When Bishoy came back, she sensed his need for a break
and refrained from asking him to resume his account.
Instead she suggested a walk in the gardens. A moment
later they stepped outside and followed the markers
leading towards the hotel swimming pool. Enhanced by
the shrill of cicadas, the heat felt pleasant after the hotel's
harsh air-conditioning. At the pool she undressed, sensing
his eyes upon her, and dived naked into the water; after
a brief hesitation he brushed off his qualms and followed
suit (there was no one there anyway). Silently she glided
towards him and took him in her arms; a long, sexy kiss
led to an underwater fumble all the more erotic for his
prodigious arousal. After indulging each other to insup-
portable heights they got out of the pool, and a moment
later he was lying on his back while she impaled herself
upon him in an overpowering release of her libido.

Next day she awoke to find him sitting at the desk, fully
dressed and with his eyes on his laptop. "Good morning,"
she mumbled, turning over on her back.

"Listen to this," he said, ignoring the comment.
"'Yesterday the Egyptian president was ordered to end

the crisis within forty-eight hours or face a military coup. His response was to disregard the hordes demanding his resignation'."

"When was that?"

"While we were having dinner." He shook his head. "If he doesn't back down it's going to end in tears, as it were." He checked his watch and turned to her. "You'd better hurry, we're meeting the driver in twenty-five minutes."

Half-an-hour later they pushed through the hotel's revolving door and got into the car. Though pregnant with the coming swelter, the heat was still bearable. For ten minutes they followed the Nile before turning right onto a big concrete bridge. The big river reminded her of a passage in Flaubert's *Voyage in the Orient*: "At times one thinks one is on a huge lake of which one does not see the edge." A cruise along the far bank led to a left turn after which they stopped before a pair of statues worn down by thousands of years of erosion. "The Colossi of Memnon, 1500 B.C.," declared Bishoy without getting out. "One of many tokens of the glory of Amenhotep III. What marvels!"

At their destination they found themselves all alone. "Hurrah for political instability!" Bishoy exclaimed as they got out. Carved into the hillside, a stone arch was flanked by a pair of plaques saying, "Ten Minutes Only in the Tomb" and "No. 66 Tomb of Queen Nefertari 19th Dyn." A man in a *gallabeya* shook their hands and led them inside. Under an Italian inscription – the site had been discovered by an archaeologist from Turin – a long ramp led down to the mausoleum proper. Hieroglyphs glinted in the penumbra; the walls showed human and animal images in immaculate condition.

While Bishoy stayed behind chatting with the guide, Kristina descended to the first platform; a mural showed a woman in a skin-tight dress holding another's hand. Presently Bishoy joined her. "That's Isis presenting Nefertari to Ptah, the god of creation and craftsmanship," he said. "What a gem!" She studied him as he stood there, her heart warming to his enthusiasm. A mass of images followed, each more pristine than the last, each described by Bishoy with an expert's eagerness: Alba, a bird with the face of the queen; the Spirit of Fertility with a scorpion on her head; Nefertari on her mummification couch crowned by the mask of Osiris. "What treasures," he repeated over and over. "What immeasurable treasures."

An hour later, driven indoors by the heat, they returned to the hotel. In her mercifully air-conditioned room, Kristina brought up her emails. There was only one, a message from her mother asking how she was doing. She replied with due reassurance before checking the latest political events. Several ministers had resigned; violence threatened the cities; the army was pledging to revoke the constitution; the country stood on the edge. After a while she lay down on the bed and shut her eyes. Instantly she was being chided by Desmond Burroughs for botching the Cairo project. "What the hell were you thinking?" he said. "The job was ours for the taking." Suddenly her office phone rang, but when she made to answer it, it wasn't her office phone at all but the one on her bedside table. Bishoy was calling to inform her that the kitchen was closing in twenty minutes, so she got up and ran a comb through her hair before joining him. When the waiter had taken her order, she watched Bishoy fill their wine glasses. "You never got to the end of your story," she said.

"I know." He took a sip and put down his glass. "I was relieved to let it go. But now I want to finish it. Remind me where I left off. Had I started on the—"

"You were getting to the end of your backgammon match."

"Ah yes." He paused again, briefly. "There was no set number of games. The first to win five got the kitty. In the end we played nine and the match took three days, or rather three nights, for we always began at midnight. Mahmoud was courtesy itself, congratulating me on my victories and offering me a drink or a glass of water whenever I looked tired. At dawn we would both sign off on the score so as to avoid any disagreement the next day. Then I would go home and sleep until lunchtime.

"On the first night we played two games, both of which I won. The second went the other way, and we might have been quits if I hadn't raised the stakes so exorbitantly. Though I ended up dangerously down, I'd never been more fired up. On the third night Mahmoud moved in for the kill. Any trace of his former chivalry yielded to his gambler's bloodlust; in an hour the match was over. In line with our deal the pool had to be doubled by the loser, which I obeyed without demurral. In the morning I wired Mahmoud his winnings before telling Hawwa I needed some time to myself. That afternoon I flew down to the Red Sea. The rest you know."

In the silence that followed, Kristina wondered how much money he had lost. Unwilling to pose so brash a question, she asked how Hawwa had reacted, at which he turned to her. He seemed to have lost track of their conversation. "I'm sorry?" he said.

"How did Hawwa react to your wish for some time off?"

He shrugged. "We'd had such moments before."

"What do you mean?"

"Needing a break; so she took it in her stride."

"Have you spoken since?"

"No."

At this point their lunch arrived, *omelette aux fines herbes* for her and grilled chicken for him. Ignoring his own while she started on hers, Bishoy said, "You'll never guess who emailed me this morning."

"Who?"

"Mahmoud."

She looked up with her fork in mid-air. This was a thunderbolt! "What for?"

"He wants a playoff."

"What's a playoff?"

"A final showdown; a revenge match."

She kept her eyes on him. "And?" she said.

"I can't do it. I haven't got the money."

For a long while she gaped. She must have misheard him. "Are you telling me you gambled away your father's entire fortune in … what, four days?"

"Three; yes, every penny of it." He lit a cigarette, his food intact. "Apart from the odd scrap in his foreign bank accounts, it's all gone."

She let her eyes skim over him: his brown complexion; his dense black eyelashes; the sexy way his shirt hugged his torso; the tremor of his hand as he raised his cigarette to his lips. After a while their waiter seemed to realise that he wasn't going to finish his food and came over to remove their plates. When the bill came, she grabbed it, brushing off his protestations, after which they returned to their separate rooms for a nap. Idly Kristina stood at the window; the sun was beating down like a celestial punishment. Slowly she shook her head. What a hero he was, this Bishoy agonistes, like a doomed pharaoh courting rack and ruin. The thought sparked a tenet of French law often quoted by her mother. *Non-assistance à personne en danger*, known in English as the Duty to Rescue, and suddenly it dawned on her that for all her elation at Bishoy's torment, observing it from the wings without trying to save him would be a moral felony.

At 5.30 they visited the Ramesseum, shrine to the eponymous pharaoh, which they toured in the evening gilt before returning to the hotel for dinner. As usual they were the only clients. Though tempted to revive the subject at hand, she thought better of it, and slowly their talk flagged. He seemed to be holding something back. After paying the bill again, this time to no objection on his part, she followed him to the bar. On the TV President Morsi was concluding a speech full of invocations to Allah the Most Merciful amid pledges to lay down his life for his office. Far from denouncing him, however, Bishoy merely muttered, "That was his swan song." Sensing disclosure in the air, Kristina kept quiet. At last, leaning back, heavy-lidded, as usual when he was hatching a statement, he said, "Mahmoud got back to me."

Her heartbeat quickened. "I trust you fobbed him off," she said, keeping her cool.

"I tried to."

"Didn't you tell him you have no money?"

"I did, but…"

"But what?" she pressed.

"He wants me to stake my flat."

She felt a tingle down her spine. "I hope you refused," she said.

"I said I'd think about it."

She leaned forward and put her hand on his. "Don't do it, Bishoy. Please be sensible. Don't do it."

## III

Past nineteenth-century façades, clusters of troops and faded advertisements for such long-gone luxuries as Cigares Coutarelli and Chaussures Lob, the cab pulled up outside a terrace filled with hookah-smoking men. Across the street an art-deco entrance was flanked by marble plaques saying Windsor Hotel and Restaurant in English on one side and Arabic on the other. After checking in she was taken up a rickety old lift to the third floor. In her room she opened the window and saw a pair of military planes drawing a huge heart against the sky. Beneath it an Arabic caption was translated by the bellboy as We Love You, Cairo. It was the army's way of winning over the people after their coup. She unpacked her computer and typed in the hotel password to find an email from Desmond Burroughs. "Dear Kristina," it said.

This is to confirm that the presentation has been scheduled for tomorrow, 5.00 p.m. at the American University.

The attached brochure has been changed at the client's request. You'll need to know it by heart in case of any unexpected questions. Remember the 3 R's: rehearse, rehearse and rehearse.

Our only competitor is a local, Shahira Fahmy. She's supposed to be very good, so be sure to rise to the occasion.

Best of luck,

Desmond

She opened the attachment and scanned its parts. Environmental Considerations, a redundant section she'd taken out before her trip, had been restored. With a surge of annoyance – why must they treat her like a baby? – she brought up the original and sent it to the hotel's email address in defiance of her boss's orders. Then she called reception and ordered five printouts. With that she folded her computer and sat back. On the night of the president's swan song she'd refrained from trying to seduce Bishoy: there would have been no point, he'd have had trouble performing. At breakfast he looked predictably drawn. "I've accepted Mahmoud's offer," he said, as she knew he would.

"Against my advice." In the pause that followed she repressed the urge to scold him. "So what's your plan?"

"We'll be playing three games. The winner of two takes all."

"So in the space of an hour you might lose your sole remaining possession."

"Yes – or settle the score."

An argument on the street pulled her from her reverie. Darkness had fallen, so she checked her watch before taking the lift to the ground floor. Presently she was pushing through a clamour of car horns and exhaust fumes and expletives. After several minutes along a dusty avenue she turned left, made her way down a shallow slope and reached a square dominated by the statue of a man in a fez. Across from the famous Groppi – once a gathering place for high society but now irreversibly run-down – a glass door said Café Riche in archaic Levantine script. Inside, waiters in Nubian costumes were weaving between the tables, too busy to pay her any heed. Suddenly an arm shot up in the corner; it was Bishoy. "Welcome to my canteen," he said, getting up and pulling out a chair when she reached him.

She sat down and surveyed the other customers. "It's nice to have company for a change," she said. "They look happy."

"This place has always been a hub of secular democracy." He hailed a waiter and asked what she wanted to drink.

"A beer, please."

He ordered two Stellas and lit a cigarette.

"So what's the plan?" she asked.

"I'm meeting with Mahmoud at midnight tomorrow." He pocketed his matches. "At my place."

"Why at your place?"

He shrugged. "To assess the stakes, I guess."

Her heart sank. For a moment she thought of trying to dissuade him before concluding that there was no point. "Why is it always midnight?" she asked instead.

"I don't know; maybe he's superstitious; the witching hour and all that."

Dinner was a decent enough shish tawook. After an hour of lackadaisical chit-chat they split the bill before stepping out and confirming their next appointment at

1.00 a.m. the next morning. Braving the heat on her way back to the hotel, she cursed her inability to rescue Bishoy from himself. Though she must act before it was too late, she had no clue how to go about it. After a nightcap in the hotel bar, she went to bed no closer to a plan of action. She had trouble falling asleep, tossing and turning like a pancake until the small hours.

At eight she awoke to a memory that had bubbled up in her sleep. The day before, on their way in from the airport, the cab had dropped Bishoy off at his home, and while waiting for the driver to take out his luggage her eye had alighted on a pair of brass plaques flanking the door. Bishoy Issa, said one, and Boutros Issa the other. Suddenly alert, she rose, washed and dressed before going downstairs for breakfast. Forty minutes later she got out of a taxi at in Zamalek; it was 9.20, perfect timing, and within moments she'd rung the relevant doorbell on the first floor. After a few seconds the door opened to the sight of a heavyset man who frowned at the sight of an unannounced stranger. "What can I do for you?" he asked coldly.

"I have come to see Mister Boutros Issa" she replied.

"What is it about?"

"His nephew Bishoy. He's in bad trouble and needs help."

Though the news must have come as a surprise, the man remained stony-faced. After a brief hesitation he let her in and took her to his study, where he bade her sit down before asking for her name and writing it down. Then he sat back and listened to her account. "Mubarak?" he asked when she'd finished. "Like the former president?"

"Correct: Mahmoud Mubarak."

He made a note of it and put down his fountain-pen. "Are you Bishoy's ... lover?" he asked with disconcerting abruptness.

"No," she said: the question was indiscreet and beside the point.

"Then why are you interceding on his behalf?"

"Isn't that what friends are for?"

At his sceptical look it struck her that he hadn't smiled once during the entire meeting. At last he got up, still poker-faced, and saw her out. She'd done what she could, she thought on her way to the taxi rank of the Marriott Hotel. Now she could but hope for the best.

## IV

To the wail of a distant police siren – the soundtrack of London, as she called it – she raised the volume of the TV. Amid scenes of violent street fighting an off-screen voice said, "In Cairo three-hundred civilians and forty-three police officers were killed earlier this morning." For the hundredth time she wondered how it would end. She did a lot of wondering these days. The day after her return from Egypt Desmond Burroughs had informed her that they'd been rejected by the British University. "It's not the first time you've gone rogue," he'd said about her omission of the page marked Environmental Considerations. "But it's the last. You will clear your desk and leave the office by noon." Since then her mind had veered from the quest for a new job to the outcome of Bishoy's story. All of a sudden, as if on cue, the ping of an email caused her to go to her desk. "Dear Kristina," she read, "I confirm my arrival at Heathrow at 15.00 tomorrow afternoon. I will be staying at the Leonardo da Vinci Hotel in Queen's Gate Gardens. Let's meet in the lobby at 8.00 p.m. Much has happened since our last meeting. With love, Bishoy."

Their last meeting ... after her presentation at the British University, she'd attended a dinner for the two competing architects before returning to her hotel for an (unsuccessful) nap. At 12.45 a.m. she directed a cab to Sheikh Zuweid Street, where she announced herself with the night porter and took the lift to the second floor. While waiting for Bishoy to let her in, she wondered if her anxiety was written on her face. Not that she had long to think about it: when he opened the door his pallor betrayed his fate as clearly as if he'd voiced it out loud.

He took her to a large living room overlooking the Nile, its waters reflecting the city lights. At his offer of a nightcap she said grappa for old times' sake; while he fussed round the drinks table she scanned the room. Dominated by a large picture of the Battle of the Pyramids and flanked by a pair of Ottoman side-tables, a bottle-green sofa stood on a Persian rug entirely covering the floor. Between bunches of flowers and black-and-white photographs from the early 1900s, every item spelled wealth and taste. "It's magnificent!" she exclaimed when Bishoy handed over her glass.

"Yes," he said laconically. "And it's gone."

While she scanned him – never was calamity as grandly proclaimed – he bent down to pick up a parcel from the table. Loosely wrapped in brown paper, it contained a copy of Dostoevsky's *Crime and Punishment*. At his prompting, she opened it; the inside cover had a handwritten legend saying, "Bishoy: do you remember the day when I had to rush home to fetch my guidebook? What I didn't tell you was that I'd left it at your place, not mine. On my way out I popped into your room to wish you good morning but you were still asleep, so I tiptoed out again." It was signed "Hawwa, July the 4th 2013."

Kristina stood there as the horror sank in. "July 4th … wasn't that…" She trailed off, unable to finish her train of thought.

"The morning after my fling with Nazli? That's right. And she was lying by my side."

"My God! But … when did Hawwa give you this?"

"She didn't. Mahmoud gave it to me after the game."

"You mean to say…" she trailed off as the terrible truth sank in.

"That the offended parties conspired to destroy the offender? Correct."

And then, suddenly, a flood inside her burst its banks in a torrent of lust blinding her to all else but its object. Pressing her body against his, she kissed him passionately, fumbling with his belt in a frenzied search for his hardness. "I want you," she gasped, kneeling down as if to eat him alive. "I need you." A moment later she was bringing him to climax before straddling him on the carpet and doing it again and then again. At dawn they lay panting in exhaustion; when at last she got up, the sun was rising over the river. "I need a cab," she said, picking up her clothes from the floor. "My plane leaves in three hours' time."

Her mind still full of these memories, she entered the Leonardo da Vinci Hotel. At the sight of her, Bishoy got to his feet, beaming. How ordinary a man looked in a suit and tie, she said to herself as she approached him. A moment later they took a cab to a restaurant called Locanda Parmigiana, where they sat down and ordered white wine before leaning back and looking at each other. "You've changed," she remarked, at which he smiled and said, "*You* haven't, you look just the same." For a while they discussed his country's politics: bombings, terrorist attacks, opposition rallies and mass-killings by Abdel al-Sisi, the new strongman.

When their drinks arrived, they sipped at them while the place filled up. After a while Kristina broke the silence. "You said you had lots to tell," she ventured when the waiter had taken their orders, causing Bishoy to sit back, eyes half-closed as was his way. (At least *that* hadn't changed.) "After you left my apartment I couldn't go back to sleep," he began. "The deal with Mahmoud required me to leave my flat and all its contents the next day but one. At four I went out. After scouring my neighbour-hood, I crossed the river and went to Khan El-Khalili, you know, the old market not far from your hotel. Qirmiz Alley, Bayt al-Qadi Square, Khan Ja'far School, for hours I basked in my heritage. By the time I got back I'd decided to throw myself into the Nile. But where? In town? In the country? In the desert? Finally I brought out a map of Cairo. I needed somewhere deep and discreet.

"And then, just as I'd identified a couple of suitable loca-tions, the door opened to the sight of my uncle Boutros entering unannounced. Skipping the small talk, he sat down and asked for a Scotch-and-water. After I'd handed it to him, he got straight to the point, enquiring what had led me to throw away my forebears' hard-earned fortune like so much disposable waste. I asked him what he meant but he interrupted me and snapped, 'Cut the waffling. I want the truth and I want it now, all of it without embellishment or omission.'

"I did as he asked, which took about ten minutes. Then I turned on the lights, for it was dark now, and handed him *Crime and Punishment*. The inscription caused him a sly little smile. 'You've been set up, *ibn akhi*,' he said. 'Set up by a woman scorned and a small-time mobster.' Then he fixed me head-on. 'In case you're wondering how I learned of your predicament, let's say that after my many decades in business I have useful ... contacts. Your gambler friend is a well-known quantity to my private investigators. Not only are his dice notoriously weighted but he uses his profits to finance his own drug ring. Which doesn't say much for the company you keep'."

The arrival of their food interrupted Bishoy's story, so they ate in silence. When he'd finished his pasta, he took a sip of wine and sat back. "Where was I?" he said. "Ah yes, Uncle Boutros. 'Listen to me,' he began. 'First thing tomorrow morning your friend Mahmoud will be ... shall we say persuaded to sign a notarised retraction of his claims in your regard or face a decade behind bars. By then you will have booked your flight to London. The Bank of Egypt have agreed to hire you at my recommendation. Your job will be to raise money for their capital management group. It'll be hard work, but hard work is what life's about. You start on July the 19th, which should give you time to find a place to stay. I'd originally earmarked you as my successor on our board of trustees. As you can imagine that's off the table now. If you turn into a dependable member of the family I might think again. I believe in second chances. But not third ones.' With that he got up, said goodnight and walked out."

A moment of silence followed. At the next table a young couple was speaking German. "What a story!" Kristina said at last.

When the waiter had cleared the table, Bishoy asked for the bill and turned back to her. "There's one thing I still haven't figured out," he said.

"What's that?"

"The speed of my uncle's reaction. Spinning such a web in a matter of hours seems to ... defy reality."

"What do you mean?" she asked disingenuously.

"No one knew about my problem except Mahmoud, Hawwa and myself – and you, of course, but by then you were six miles high. I still can't fathom how he found out about it. It's almost uncanny."

"It does sound odd."

He shook his head in lingering disbelief. "In any case I intend to regain my uncle's confidence." He put his hand on hers. "And I'm hoping you'll help me do so." He paused as if expecting a reaction. When none came, he said, "Shall we go to my hotel for a nightcap?"

"I can't," she lied, using the arrival of their bill as a pretext to remove her hand. "I have an early interview in the City."

Outside, an unseasonable chill hung in the air. "I can drop you off if you like," he said.

"No thanks, I'll make my own way." She hailed a black cab and watched it pull up. "Goodnight Bishoy." He tried to kiss her on the lips but she turned away and got into the taxi. En route to her flat the radio intoned a song by B.B. King. *The Thrill Is Gone, The thrill is gone away…*

# Old Walt

## I

If ever there were a specimen of what is known as idle wealth, or, in Communist jargon, social parasitism, it was Walter Kershaw, descendant in the junior line of Lord Gilling (1711–80), whose sugar plantations in Jamaica secured him the unimaginable wealth that would later be squandered by his progeny. Until Walter's father married Ruth Ochs, scion of one of America's most powerful industrial dynasties, his forebears had endured an impoverishment all the more inexorable for their reluctance to do anything about it (except make it worse). Walter, or Old Walt as he would come to be known, had a very different fate: at thirty, eight years after his wedding and several decades before I met him, he inherited his mother's fortune. With the lean years now gone and the family fortunes back on track, he refused to embrace such middle-class pursuits as industry or finance – least of all, perish the thought, philanthropy! Fun and fun alone, in its most aristocratic and futile forms, would be his goal, and soon he was basking in the nobleman's most worthless pursuits, the field and the turf. Not that it made him unlikeable to me, on the contrary. After all, the indulgence of one's every whim often makes for a cheerful disposition. And so it did with Old Walt.

Of all his foibles, the most notorious was his sexual avidity. Since his teens he would close in on any halfway

decent-looking female of child-bearing age without both-
ering to establish her interest in advance. Any smile or
bland compliment such as "Lovely to see you" or "You
look well" would be taken as a come-on, and though
stories abounded of his harassment, his charm often let
him get away with it. Even his marriage to the elegant
Joanne Clark, friend to the Duchess of Windsor and dop-
pelgänger of Marlene Dietrich, failed to stop him from
trying his luck every chance he got, all the more so for
his wife's propensity to turn a blind eye. (In those days
women still bought into the adage that boys will be boys.)

Aged nineteen and twenty-one respectively, Rosie and
I had yet to get engaged when she took me to "Grampa's
place," as she called Rye Bury, Walter and Joanne's manor
house in East Sussex. Though the realisation that we were
childhood sweethearts must have tainted his first impression of me – he had looked forward to a more glittering
match for his pretty granddaughter – he was brought
around by my suggestive sense of humour. I recall his
roars of laughter at my story about Cassius Clay, the
black boxer later to change his name to Mohammed Ali.
Informed at a restaurant in Alabama that they didn't serve
Negroes, he quipped, "That's okay, I don't eat Negroes!"
After that the old man would welcome me into his home
with raucous cordiality.

For all his faults, I cannot deny my fondness for Old
Walt; his jollity was somehow disarming. In later years
his increasing deafness spawned some hilarious moments.
A case in point harked back to a dinner at Wilton's on
Jermyn Street, his favourite restaurant. At one point his
youngest daughter – my mother-in-law, for by then I was

married to Rosie – embarked on a story about one of her friends. While speeding down the M5 a few days before, she'd run into a stray horse, its hoof crashing through her windscreen. "Not a bone in her face was left intact," was the shocking conclusion. At Old Walt's blithe air, Granny, as I now called Joanne, leaned forward to put him right. But it was not to be. With a blithe air, as if it were the best story he'd heard in his life, he gulped down some claret and cried, "Well I'm delighted to hear it!"

Less endearing was Old Walt's handling of his underlings. Not content with ogling the younger maids and extolling their curves while they were within earshot, he would treat his manservants like serfs. Two instances spring to mind as I write. The first bears on his daily horse rides across the estate, often with Rosie and me in tow. One day the three of us emerged from the woods to the sight of a fenced meadow stretching out before us. Unlike our former jaunts, its gate was padlocked this time, and one of the keepers, who happened to be at hand, offered to unlock it and let us through. Chafing at the bit to vanquish the beckoning expanse, our horses flared their nostrils with loud snorts, whinnying nervously and scraping the earth with their hoofs. But Old Walt held back. "Whose is this field, Morris?" he snapped at the keeper. "Is it mine?"

"I'm afraid not, Sir. It's mine."

"What are you talking about? This field belongs to the estate!"

"I'm afraid not, Sir," the keeper repeated. "It's my field. I inherited it from my father."

"Stuff and nonsense, Morris!" cried Walter, red-faced,

and I recall the incongruity of a man who had never lifted a finger in his life begrudging his dependent so modest a possession.

"Excuse me, Sir," said the keeper. "I'm not Morris. I'm Williams."

"*What the hell has that got to do with anything?*" the old man bellowed. "Now open that gate and let us through!"

The other episode occurred at lunch a week later. It was a beautiful day; the dining room glowed with summer sparkle; birds twittered outside the open window. In addition to the hosts there were six elderly guests as well as Rosie and I. While being served his entrée by Birtwistle, the butler, who was prone to the occasional tipple, Old Walt suddenly looked up and declared "The man stinks!" for all the world as if the man wasn't there. Fleetingly I wondered if he would hurl the soup tureen in his master's face. But he didn't, he merely flushed dark red and carried it out, to his employer's blithe oblivion.

Late next morning Old Walt was sitting in his study when he heard a knock on the door. No doubt to his surprise, his usual barked "Come!" led to Birtwistle and the entire staff including the keepers, Morris and Williams, to step in. "There's somefing we need to tell yer," said the latter when the last maid had shut the door behind her. No greeting, no apology for the disturbance, no Sir or Mister Kershaw or any of the deference traditionally reserved between servant and employer. "If you look out the window you'll see a pair o' vans bein' loaded wiv luggage."

The old man did so. "So what?" he said, turning back to the keeper.

"The girls are disgusted by the way you ogle them like a dirty old man and the rest of us 'ave 'ad it up to 'ere wiv bein' bossed around or tyken for someone else or told they stink wiv never a please or a fank you."

Old Walt glared at him. "What are you talking about?" he said after a moment.

"We quit. That's what I'm talking about. All of us, the 'ole staff wivout exception. Now."

Though the news must have come as something of a jolt – it was the middle of summer and the house full of guests – he kept it to himself, merely veering his eyes from one rebel to the other like the barrels of a shotgun. At last he said, "See if I care."

Birtwistle gave an ominous smile. "You might yet change yer mind about that."

"You don't say."

"Yeah. We're launchin' a class action against you."

"What for?" Old Walt sneered. "Overpaying you?"

"Workplace 'arassment, they call it."

"Get out!" was the answer. Then, pointing over their heads, "There's the door."

One by one they did so with Williams at the rear. From the doorway, no doubt buoyed by his new-found emancipation, he turned around with a little wink and said, "See you in court, mate!"

The days to come unfolded in stark contrast to Rye Bury's usual luxuriousness. The guests were asked to make their own beds, wash their bathtubs and empty the ashtrays in the drawing room before turning in. The King's Head, a local gastro pub and caterer, was to hired to deliver lunch and dinner. Rosie made breakfast since no one else knew how to boil an egg. Within a few days, to everyone's surprise, a pretty village girl named Olivia applied for the job of dishwasher. Soon I noticed her sexy smile whenever she passed Old Walt in the corridor.

## II

All the while the old man was leading his life in wilful blindness of the Damocles Sword hanging over him. He'd done nothing wrong, he would declare, he was rich and well connected and his accusers knew better than to run afoul of him. A week or so later he was jolted into (fleeting) sobriety by a solicitor's letter from Derby Row in London. To avoid any further trouble, it said, half a year's salary settled to each of the plaintiffs within a week would cause them to drop their suit. Failing that, his misbehaviour would be laid bare in court and in the press. Though it was a large sum, Old Walt could easily have paid it but for his unwillingness to "kow-tow to a bunch of freeloaders out for a quick buck." Next day he sent them a sheet of writing paper headed Rye Bury, Sussex, and stamped with the words DROP DEAD in big red capital letters.

None of which caused me any particular surprise – by now I was accustomed to the old man's eccentric ways – beyond a sort of reluctant admiration for his dogged self-sabotage. At the end of my summer holiday, and with only a few days left before my return to university, I sensed an insidious discomfort behind his jaunty exterior. Meanwhile Olivia, the new girl, had been assigned to cook breakfast and make the beds, while I was charged with the drinks and wine cellar.

On my last day but one I found the larder empty of

wine, so I fetched a few bottles from the cellar; next morning, to my surprise, they, too, were gone, so I went back to replenish the stock. On my return I heard scuffling and protestations from a servant's room under the stairs. The door stood ajar, so I peeped in to find Old Walt pinning Olivia against the wall while yanking at his zipper with the evident intention of having his way with her. No sooner had she spotted me than she pushed him off while I scuttled into one of the rooms off the corridor, making sure to keep the door ajar. Seconds later I saw her race upstairs with her attacker in panting pursuit. Needless to say I kept the episode to myself, and next day I left for Cambridge and the start of the Michaelmas term.

A couple of weeks later I received a letter from H.M. Courts and Tribunals Service headed Witness Summons.

You are summoned to attend at

Ground Floor
Victory House
30–34 Kingsway
London
WC2

on

Monday, November 12, 2012, at 10.00 am (and each following day of the hearing until the court tells you that you are no longer required) to give evidence in respect of a class action suit against Walter Anthony Kershaw of Rye Bury Hall, Rye Bury, East Sussex,

BN32. This summons is issued on the application of the prosecution's legal counsel, Morley and Slade (London).

The sum of £50 is paid or offered to you with this summons. This is to cover your travelling expenses and includes an amount by way of compensation for loss of time.

If you do not comply with this summons, you will be liable to a fine. Furthermore, disobedience of a Witness Summons is seen as criminal contempt of court and punishable by up to a year in prison. You may also be liable to pay any wasted costs that may arise because of your non-compliance.

My inferences after reading it twice sprang instantly to mind: one, that my cross-examination would bear on Walter's scuffle with Olivia; and two, that I lacked any experience with the law. So I rang my father and asked him to make an appointment with our family solicitor. His messages when I met him struck me for their pitiless clarity: that lying under oath, known as perjury, is a crime punishable by jail; and that my testimony would spell Old Walt's downfall as inexorably as day turns to night.

At the Royal Courts of Justice I was shown to a bench outside the courtroom and told to wait my turn. When at last I was called in, I saw a female judge facing the defence and prosecution barristers from a raised dais; behind them a pair of secretaries were taking notes. From the dock, Old Walt gave me a deadpan look. As I took my post in the witness box, I spotted all of Rye Bury's staff, among them Olivia, Birtwistle and both keepers, in the audience. No sooner had I taken the so-called oath of affirmation than I was addressed by a hostile prosecution barrister. "Did you go to the cellar of Rye Bury Hall on September 14th?" he asked with no greeting or traditional niceties.

"Yes," I said.

"For what purpose?"

"To fetch some wine."

"Describe the sequel."

My palms moistening, I kept quiet.

"I said describe the sequel."

I furrowed my brow. "Are you referring to—"

"I'm referring to what you saw on your way back from the cellar."

"I don't understand."

"*What's not to understand?*" he barked. "It's a simple question! You went to the cellar to fetch some wine. What did you see on your way back?"

And then, all of a sudden, the pennies that had been teasing me in the last couple of days began dropping one by one. First, that the whole thing had been a set-up, including Olivia's application for the job, her glad-eying of Old Walt and the wine's removal from the pantry aimed at roping in the only legally non-family member of the household (Rosie and I had yet to get engaged). Second that attempted rape is a far worse felony than generic workplace harassment. And third, most fateful of all, that I held Old Walt's fate in my hands.

"Well?" barked the barrister.

Again I dithered. Over and over the words of my father's solicitor kept buffeting my mind: that perjury is a serious crime punishable by jail. With no choice but to tell the truth, I continued to play for time. "What was your question again?" I asked.

"*Come on!*" the man snapped. "This isn't a proposition from Wittgenstein. It's a simple question. What happened on your way back from the cellar?"

And then, suddenly, the clincher that had been staring me in the face revealed itself in all its simplicity: that coming from the only witness to Old Walt's crime, my statement could not be corroborated or denied except by Olivia, whose bias nullified her credibility. At the same time I heard my voice speak out like an alien organ untethered to my will. "I saw nothing on my way back from the cellar," it said, loud and clear.

Now it was the prosecutor's turn to gape. "What d'you mean you saw nothing?" he asked.

"Nothing untoward."

"Let me remind you that you are under oath, young man."

"I'm aware of that."

"And yet you persist in your lie?"

"Are you calling me liar?" I taunted.

"Correct! You're a—"

"*Prove it!*" At his stony silence I repeated my taunt. "Go on, prove it!"

Only then did it dawn on him that he'd been appointed to represent a calculated intrigue; and that challenging my statement would merely show up his clients as the scammers they were. As if on cue the judge asked him if he had any proof to back up his claim that I had lied. "Real proof," she added. "Not conjecture or hearsay or the claim of an interested party." Rattled, he conceded that he hadn't, so she told him to sit down. For a moment or two the hearing limped on before finally giving up the ghost. By overshooting their mark the accusers were left empty-handed and Old Walt strolled off scot-free.

### III

The most notable upshot of Old Walt's acquittal was a complete shift in his behaviour towards his staff. No sooner had a new team been hired than he would greet them by name with such cries of "Smithson, are you well?" or "Martina, how's the family?" Soon it dawned on me that his past sins derived less from his character or personality than from the entitlement that comes with too much money too soon. In the decade after my marriage to Rosie he proved as kind a great-grandfather as could be, ever ready with presents and silly stories for the children. When Granny died in 1992, we attended her funeral at Rye Bury followed by Old Walt's five years later. In its wake we heard that he had left his assets equally among his children except for the house, which went 50-50 to "my granddaughter Rosie and her loyal husband Basil Culpepper."

# THE MAHARANI OF DYALPURA

## I

One evening in April 2013 I went to meet a friend at a café in the Brixton market. It was a lovely day, all sunshine and trees in bloom, and after escaping the Delhi swelter as I do every year, I revelled in the pleasure of an English spring. As I sat there a waitress came out to take my order. She'd approached me from inside the restaurant, so we couldn't see each other's faces till she was standing in front of me. Reflex thoughts battered my mind at the sight of her. First, the fleeting panic of seeing someone you ought to remember but don't; second, a frisson of recognition at the unkempt figure looking down at me; and finally, the realisation that she was suffering the same perplexity.

The sequel unfolded in quick succession. A moment after re-entering the restaurant she came back in a raincoat, strode down the gallery and vanished in the crowd without so much as a glance my way. At this point my friend's arrival sent the episode to the back of my mind, so it was only in the taxi an hour later that the penny dropped. Frantically I knocked on the cab's glass partition and asked to be taken back to the Brixton market. Inside the café I asked the manager about the Indian waitress who'd served me – or rather hadn't – earlier on. Did he know who I meant? "Sure I do," he said. "Samaira Patel and she's done a runner."

My heart leapt. Samaira – so it was true! "Can you tell me where she lives?" I asked.

He gave me a quizzical look. "I shouldn't really," he said.

"She's an old friend of mine."

He shrugged. "All right then." He opened a file and rummaged through its contents. "'Ere it is: Montevideo Hotel, 223 Cromwell Road."

Desperate to get to her before it was too late, I hastened down the arcade and hailed another taxi. Half an hour later, at the reception of a seedy bed-and-breakfast in South Kensington I learned that Samaira Patel had checked out an hour ago, destination unknown.

## II

My name is Sanjay IV, twelfth Maharajah of Rajpurwada, and at the time of these events I was thirty-eight years old. Like many of my peers my education had a decidedly British imprint: six years at Blandford School in Kent, a favourite among Indian royals, led me to Balliol College, Oxford. Meanwhile, generations of indulgence had so depleted my family's fortune that after gaining my degree I became its first member to face the grindstone. I opted for the antiques trade, which I knew a little about, and after a six-month stint at a gallery on Mount Street I decided to open a shop in Delhi's antiques quarter, Sunder Nagar. By then I knew Samaira.

Our meeting harked back to the aftermath of my father's death two years earlier. Having supervised his cremation and the settlement of his labyrinthine estate, I had booked my return flight to London. The night before, I'd joined a few friends at one of those diners on Connaught Place that crop up from time to time only to disappear just as fast. Later a group of us went to a bar named Lord of the Drinks, and next morning I woke up by myself. All I could recall was drinking much too much and going to bed ridiculously late. As I lay there with a pounding headache, it dawned on me that I hadn't slept alone. Only after three aspirins and a strong coffee did it hit me. Of course! Samaira, Crown Princess of Dyalpura, youngest-ever member of Rajasthan's Legislative Assembly, who'd had to catch an early train home.

Back in London I heard nothing about her for several months until one day a mutual friend gave me her details at a summer party in London. But when I dialled her number her mobile phone went repeatedly to voicemail. So I rang her landline only to hear that she was away and wouldn't be back until further notice. By the time of my move to Delhi I'd forgotten all about her until one day at a drinks party in Nizamuddin East I felt a tap on my shoulder and turned around. It was Samaira with a big smile. "Well, well, well," I cried, kissing her on both cheeks. "It's been a while."

"Indeed it has," she said. "Three years, to be precise."

My first reaction was to wonder what I'd seen in her. Short, sallow and tending to plumpness, she had nothing of the lovelies embellishing the pages of India's gossip columns. Combined with an impatience bordering on conceit, it should by rights have stifled any wish for more. Yet there was something about her, a sort of sweetness deliberately suppressed. Only by her smile did she reveal it. "I tried to call you a few years ago," I said, "but you'd done a disappearing act."

She wobbled her head. "Sometimes one must assert one's independence."

"Quite right," I answered, unwilling to seem put out.

At this point we were offered a platter of soft drinks; after picking up a pineapple juice Samaira lowered her voice. "If I'd known there'd be a ban on booze I'd have stayed home," she said.

"So would everyone else," I answered. "Judging by the looks on their faces."

"Why is it that Muslims always impose their precepts on others? If they want to abstain, let them, but what's it got to do with me?"

"Don't," I said. We were guests and courtesy obliged.

After a while we decided to go to the Imperial Hotel for a nightcap. In the bar we sat down under a picture of the old Maharajah of Orchha. "What a character," I said, pointing out his bemedalled breast and bristling white beard. "Those were the days."

"I disagree," Samaira retorted. "I don't believe in inherited rank. Every man for himself."

"Coming from you?"

Her eyes flashed. "Have I no right to an opinion just because I'm a royal?" she snapped. "Ever since the abolition of the Privy Purses we've had to fend for ourselves. And so it should be. We're in the twenty-first century, for God's sake."

"If you say so."

"Look at *me*," she insisted. "Since firing my advisors I've made more money than all of them put together."

"A calm sea does not a skilled sailor make," I muttered in reference to the docile stock market.

In the silence that followed I wondered if I'd offended her. If so, I never found out, for at this point we were joined by a group of mutual friends and the subject fell by the wayside. All I recall is nodding off to the twitter of the awakening birds; with Samaira beside me for the second time.

In the morning I lay there, recalling the night before to the sound of her steady breathing. Within seconds of my front door falling shut she'd assaulted me like a tigress on heat, devouring me as if to swallow me whole before throwing off her clothes and vaulting me with a swivelling motion such as I'd ever known before. When she woke up she seemed to wonder where she was, but no sooner had the penny dropped than she set out to dispel any suspicion that the night before had been a fluke. At last, her lust quenched, she washed and got dressed before leaving for the station with a vague wave of her hand, as if the whole thing had been a bodily need, a hygienic release.

### III

Samaira Dyalpura is the daughter of the seventeenth Maharajah of that state. Unlike most Indian royals, whose succession rests on male primogeniture, her family lets it pass through the female line absent a male sibling. Being an only child, she'd become Maharani ten months before the events just described. Keen, quick-witted and impulsive, she took control of her fortune with no concern for any ruffled feathers. In the days after our last encounter, she crossed my mind more often than my past romances. In the end I threw caution to the nettles, rang her up and asked if I could visit her that weekend. She agreed.

At noon on Friday I boarded a train on the Delhi Cantonment and reached Dyalpura in the dark. After elbowing my way through the usual smells of an Indian railway station I was met by Samaira's driver, who loaded my luggage in the boot of an ancient Lincoln Continental and set off through sinuous alleyways, painted façades and errant cows. In the centre of town, a narrow *gali* led to the palace courtyard, from where a dimly lit staircase alighted on an endless corridor hung with battle scenes and turbaned ancestors. In my suite I washed and shaved and put on my velvet jacket before following my attendant to a small sitting room on the floor below. Samaira's welcome was typically curt. With a peck on the cheek she asked an attendant to fetch me a drink and sat down for some idle small talk.

At dinner I watched her mistreat her servants between bouts of consulting her BlackBerry. At ten I got up and bade her goodnight: if she wished to play hard to get, I was game. Next day I found a note on my breakfast tray. "At 11.30 you will be taken around the fort," it said bossily. "Lunch will be served in the rose garden at one. See you then." At the stated time I was collected by a Sikh with a big white moustache. Wide-eyed, I followed him through throne rooms, durbar halls, terraces, pavilions, en-suite courtyards, galleries of mirrors, temples to family gods and *chhatris* in jumbled profusion. Never were restraint, or symmetry, so brashly flouted nor grandeur as unabashedly displayed.

At the end of my tour I was led to a table set for two in a recess of the garden. Hearing my footsteps on the gravel she bade me take my seat and asked me about the morning. "Superb," I gushed, prompting a very sweet smile. After pouring me a glass of mineral water she clapped her hands to summon the butler and order lunch. As the meal unfolded she described her family: her mother's kindness; her late father's ailments; the infirmity of her grandmother, who lived in a nearby town. At the mention of it, her eyes lit up. "I have an idea," she said. "Why don't we go to Rajvathi for the night."

"Rajvathi?" I couldn't place it but it rang a bell.

"You know, the Emerald City."

"Of course!" I remembered its green façades. "How far is it from here?"

"Not far at all. Three-quarters of an hour to ninety minutes depending on the traffic. We could stay at my grandfather's hunting lodge, which my uncle has turned into a hotel. On the way we'll pass by some interesting landmarks." She kept her eyes on me. "Well? Are you up for it?"

"Very much so."

"Excellent!" She flashed her pretty smile. "You won't regret it."

## IV

Our excursion began with a cluster of seventeenth-century temples, all onion domes and gaudy pictures of the gods. Wild-looking sadhus begged for alms at the entrances; worshippers jostled each other under images of Ganesh and Shiva and Lakshmi; from time to time the maharani would be recognised and bowed to with due deference. We might have been in the Middle Ages. After an hour we set off again, this time for an abandoned hilltop fortress that Samaira was trying to sell to a global hotel chain. Its access being impassable by car, we got out and trudged up a slope flanked by tumbledown crenellations flickering in the foliage.

At the top of the hill a massive archway led into a court-yard overrun with untended shrubbery. Crumbling walls seemed vulnerable to the next gust of wind. We turned right, took a shallow flight of stairs towards the edge of the compound – and gasped! Far below, in a vision dotted with toy-sized cenotaphs, mini-mosques and a small Hindu temple, the Rajasthani plain stretched into the distant horizon. Elated, I turned to Samaira; her eyes were shining. "If this is heaven it's good enough for me," she said. For the first time in our liaison she seemed unre-strictedly happy.

The sun was setting when we reached Rajvathi, its emerald façades emitting the iridescent shimmer that gives it its fame. In the old town we admired the *haveli* of Samaira's grandmother but refrained from going in. ("She's too old for unannounced guests.") At her uncle's hunting-lodge-turned-hotel we were put up in the so-called royal quarters, a large pink-and-black suite with multi-coloured glass and a mural of Vishnu the Preserver. The restaurant was hung with deer antlers and stuffed boar's heads; we placed our orders and asked for a vodka-tonic each. While Samaira was regaling me with the military feats of her forebears, I sensed her to be playing for time, and no sooner had our drinks arrived than she proved me right. "There's something I need to get off my chest," she said, taking a sip and putting down her glass. "I've never told this to anyone, so please keep it to yourself."

"I promise."

She paused, looking oddly fragile. "Have you ever met my late father's sister Priti?" she said.

"I don't think so."

"You'd remember her if you had. She's known as the most difficult woman in India, rude, entitled and even, rumour has it, corrupt. She lives in London with her husband, a Brazilian diplomat called Alfredo Pinto, and their son Duranjaya, known as Duran. By family law he is my heir as the eldest male pretender." In the pause that followed she seemed to be hatching more. At last she said, "Have you ever heard of the Tiger's Heart?"

I knitted my brow in puzzlement; it was a strange question. "No," I said.

"The Tiger's Heart is a ruby from Burma worth hundreds of millions of rupees," she began. "The Emperor Aurangzeb gave it to one of my ancestors in return for his support in the Bundela War. If, as some have it, it surpasses the Hope Ruby, it would be the most valuable such stone in the world. In addition to its monetary value, it is known for a weird, almost magical property." She paused for evident effect. "At dusk on a clear day it takes on the colour of sunset, even indoors."

There was a moment of silence as a couple of tourists passed by our table. When the coast was clear, Samaira resumed her story. "One day shortly before my father's death, he sent for me," she said. "He was in his study with my aunt Priti. The reason for our summons came as something of a thunderclap. After due reflection he had decided to leave the Tiger's Heart not to me, the future Maharani, but to his only sister. After his death I was to hand it to her in person. Being young and naïve I repressed my concerns and agreed, though later I asked him by what right he was letting our family's most valuable object slip through our fingers. His answer struck me as quizzical: that one day I would thank him. For what? I pressed. 'Appeasing your aunt,' he replied."

At this point in Samaira's story, our first courses arrived. For a moment the waiters fussed around our table, removing empty vodka glasses and filling new ones with beer. When they were done I asked Samaira why her aunt needed to be appeased: wasn't the succession set in stone by centuries of tradition? Or was I missing something? "No, no, you're not missing anything, but that's not the point."

"Then what *is* the point?"

"The point is that she has a son and I don't. As a result, she feels the estate should go straight to Duran as the next male heir. What she—"

"You mean jump a generation?"

"Exactly. But what she doesn't realise, or chooses not to realise, is that our founding document, the Dyalpura Statute, which was settled by my great-uncle and amended by my father some five years before his death, names me as his successor followed by my eldest son with no ifs or buts about it. Only if I die without issue, which it's a bit premature to assume, do the title and estate go to Duran." At this point she paused while the waiters delivered our main courses.

When they'd gone she resumed her story. "At this point my father crossed the room and opened an invisible segment of its panelling to reveal a secret stairway to the cellar. At the bottom he led us down a long corridor to what looked like a blank brick wall but proved on closer inspection to have an invisible cubby-hole. In it, enclosed by a metal box wrapped in a thick velvet fabric, lay the Tiger's Heart. No one on earth had any idea of its hiding place except him and now the two of us. The only reason he was laying it bare before his death was to enable its transfer without the need for written instructions." Samaira took a sip of wine. "Two months later he expired, so I took Priti to the hideout like a good niece. It took me a while to find it, but after a moment of panic, I did so – and gasped. The recess was empty and the jewel gone!"

"*What?*" I shook my head. "But…" Silenced by shock, it took me a while to put my question into words. "Had you been followed into the cellar the first time?"

"Impossible."

"It's the only explan—"

"Impossible," she repeated, vigorously shaking her head. "There was no one there."

For a moment I sat there. "So how did Priti react?"

"Very calmly. She neither raised her voice nor expressed any outrage. She merely said that the item had been in my safekeeping and its loss was thus on me. If I didn't hand it over within a week, she would take me to court. Clearly there was nothing I could do except swear I was innocent and search for it high and low."

"And?"

"Nothing. Not a jing-bang sign of it across the length and breadth of the house."

"And now she's suing you."

"Exactly."

"Has there been a trial?"

"Not yet, but it's on the anvil. A week ago my lawyers told me that they can't put it off for much longer." A fly landed on her hand but she didn't notice. "What no one knows save the interested parties – and now you – is that barring a godsend I shall be forced to flog off half my assets or go under."

For a while I kept quiet, lamenting the incidence of such conflicts. Though few were as dramatic as Samaira's, almost every royal family had a similar story. "It's sad how so many of us fall out over inheritance," I said at last.

"Where there's a will there's a litigation," she retorted laconically.

By the end of dinner we'd polished off a bottle of wine on top of our vodkas, and within minutes of entering our suite we were grappling each other with a lustfulness all the more heated for our lengthy abstinence. Presently we did it again, though this time she was all restraint, teasing me with a languor and dexterity very unlike the frenzy of our earlier encounter. Next morning I woke up to find the shutters outlined against the curtains, hinting at a sunny day. Unwilling to disturb her, I tiptoed to the bathroom and brushed my teeth before returning to find her awake with a come-hither smile. After another bout of lovemaking she had a shower while I lay there to the languid sounds of the Rajasthani spring: twittering birds, grating cicadas, pebbles being raked on the path under our window…

On our way back to Dyalpura, Samaira made no mention of her problem, almost as if she'd got it off her chest and could move on. After lunch in her private dining room she had to attend to some local politicians, so I went to my room for a nap.. As I lay there I let my fancy take flight. Marriage to Samaira would merge our titles, making her the Maharani of Rajpurwada and Dyalpura and our son, if we had one, heir to both dynasties. At six I was awoken by a tap on the door. It was a man come to advise me that her Highness would have to bunk dinner. Wondering why, I took a stroll around the garden, ate a solitary paneer makhani in the dining room and finished my book, Nirad Chaudhuri's *A Passage to England*. In the morning I packed my suitcase and carried it to the breakfast room to find Samaira looking visibly drawn. "I'm so sorry about last night," she said, pouring me a cup of tea. "Believe me, I'd much rather have spent it with you."

"I'm sure we'd have found a way to pass the time," I answered saucily.

She ignored the comment. "The fact is, I had an unpleasant encounter with my rival in last year's election," she said.

"What happened?"

She sprinkled salt on her soft-boiled egg. "The campaign was very rough-and-tumble with no lack of personal attacks. Throughout, he accused me of every misdeed in the book. As the insults grew, I vowed to get my own back. When I won the election, I did so." She gave me a grim smile. "I showed him who was boss."

I looked at her. "What d'you mean?"

She swallowed a mouthful of egg and wiped her lips. "He was the local barber. Both his workplace and residence were in a building owned by my estate. After my victory I threw him out. From one day to the next he was unemployed and homeless."

"*What?*" I gaped at her with my knife in mid-air.

"I crushed him as he deserved and now he's stirring trouble," she replied with a nasty grin.

"What are you talking about?"

She tilted her head disagreeably. "I have a doubt," she said. "Which part of 'I crushed him' don't you get?"

"I get it, but what for?"

"Crossing me, that's what. All's fair in love and war."

"This isn't war. It's democracy."

"Not here it's not. In Dyalpura my word is law."

I looked at her in disbelief; this was a side of her I hadn't suspected. "You mean to tell me you destroyed a man for the hell of it?"

She looked at me as if to say, "What are you going to do about it?" By now my feelings for her had gone from loving affection to something more like distaste. At last, despairing of a straight answer, I shrugged and checked my watch. My train was leaving in twenty minutes' time, and when her driver came to collect me I bade her goodbye with thanks for her hospitality.

So firmly did the affair put a lid on our relationship that by the time of my trip to London I had virtually forgotten about her. Only at a party in Belgravia did she come back to me. At the sight of a grey-haired Indian woman stepping in, I asked my host who she was and heard that it was Priti Pinto, Samaira's evil aunt! Titillated, I followed her to the buffet and sat down close enough to eavesdrop on her conversation. At one point she was joined by the editor of a financial weekly who lowered his voice and muttered "We're looking into Marsupial" in reference to a hedge fund I'd vaguely heard of. Knowing little of high finance and caring less, I quickly lost interest, and when the host tapped me on the shoulder with the words "Come and meet Bollywood's latest heartthrob, Shakti Surnilla," I willingly complied.

V

By the time of my sighting of Samaira Patel, as she now called herself, in the Brixton market, what the press called the Dyalpura affair had long vanished from the headlines. After my failed mission to her hotel on the Cromwell Road, I wondered if I would see her again: having chosen one of India's most common surnames she'd be impossible to hunt down except by the sort of fluke that happens to others but never to oneself. Such were my considerations as I entered the hall of my apartment house to be handed an envelope by the doorman. Idly noting its bulkiness, I let myself into my flat and cut it open. "Dear Sanjay," I read after sitting down,

When I first read about your engagement to 'the lovely Shakti Surnilla,' I must admit to a pang of jealousy. She's out of his league, I said to myself before recalling your prowess between the sheets. I answer to a new name now: not officially, of course, that would have defeated the purpose, but by a set of fake papers. This has secured me a bit of privacy after the nightmare of the Dyalpura affair.

Though one never knows where to begin a personal story, I have opted for the day of our return to Dyalpura from Rajvathi. After lunch you went to your room for a nap while I met with a group of politicians. All of which you know already, I am merely setting the stage. What you *don't* know, or not in any detail, is my reason for bunking dinner. At breakfast I touched on it, and the time has now come to put you fully in the picture.

After seeing off the politicians in the big courtyard, I was heading back to my quarters when I was accosted by one of those ash-covered sadhus that riddle India. Young and gaunt with a nose ring and dark-grey kohl round his eyes, he looked all the more frightening for a denim jacket slung over his shoulders. I clapped my hands for someone to throw him out, but no one came, perhaps because they were afraid of him. When I tried to move on, he blocked me. 'You have sullied your dharma,' he hissed nastily. 'The dharma of your station is to protect, but you have chosen to destroy.' Approaching to within an inch of my face, he whispered, 'A curse be upon you, *kutiya* (bitch). Let what you did to me befall you too.' Only then did I recognise him as the barber I had wreaked my vengeance on three years earlier.

Before continuing, I must hark back to the wake of my inheritance. My first act was to review my liquid securities, mainly low-risk deposits and government bonds. Seeing them to be treading water, I ordered my asset managers to switch to high-octane equity and hedge funds. When they balked, I fired them all and took charge of my portfolio. One day I was introduced to what my banker called the magic of leverage, using borrowed money to boost perfor-mance, so I mortgaged all my properties and invested the proceeds alongside the rest.

Meanwhile the Indian stock market was continuing its

unstoppable rally, and soon I was strutting around Delhi like a guru of high finance. Even when the Sensex had its first big correction, I saw it as an opportunity to 'buy the dip,' in the experts' expression – except it wasn't a dip, it heralded the worst crash in history of the Bombay Stock Exchange. In the end, having raked in two years of interest from the loans they'd themselves recommended, the bankers threatened to repossess my entire estate unless I paid up within days, which I couldn't do.

And then, like the cavalry in a western, along came the most startling of friends in need: Priti Pinto. Priti Pinto? I hear you cry – my Nemesis, my Evil Aunt, my Cruella de Vil? Your surprise is all the more justified for her just having started her suit against me. By now I had more or less stopped sleeping, and whenever the phone rang I would jump out of my skin expecting some new horror. So the sound of Priti Auntie's voice came almost as a relief. Could she come for lunch the next day, she asked in her most honeyed tones: she had something to discuss with me. Sure, I replied, and at 12.30 she sailed in with a mask of gentleness that should have raised my suspicions.

The reason for her visit, she explained over lunch, involved her recent divorce from Alfredo Pinto. Having been sentenced to pay him his alimony in a lump sum by the end of the year, she was in need of ready cash. For a moment I thought she wanted a loan and almost laughed. 'Don't worry,' she said as if reading my mind. 'I'm not asking for money. On the contrary, I'm here to make you a proposal that might be in both our interests.' She paused without taking her eyes off me. 'Are you familiar with Marsupial Capital?'

Today Marsupial is a byword for fraud, but in those days it was the best-kept secret in money management. Huge and steady as a rock, it had been closed to new investors for two decades. After showing me their year-to-date returns – an amazing 17 per cent as against my negative 33 – she got to the point. 'In recent years, Marsupial's performance has made it the largest holding of my portfolio,' she said. 'As a result I have decided to cash it in and use the proceeds for Alfredo's alimony. The problem is that it has an annual lock-up period and six-month notice, which prevents me from seeing the colour of my money until the end of next year. So I'm offering to sell you my stake at net asset value: the whole jing-bang lot of it at no premium, no subscription-fee, no waiting period, nothing.'

I remember my heart jumping at her words. It was like a dream come true: not only had I longed to invest in Marsupial since the day I inherited, but it looked like the solution to all my woes. And then came the clincher. 'If you accept my offer I shall immediately withdraw my lawsuit over the Tiger's Heart. The time has come to put our differences behind us.' When she held out her hand for me to shake, I took it with a mixture of triumph and gratitude, and an hour later, alone in my living room, I raised my glass to the ancestors hanging on the wall of my living room. In the days and weeks to come I sold all my remaining liquid securities and acquired her share of Marsupial lock, stock and barrel.

On January the 14th 2008 an eight-month investigation by the editor of the British monthly *The World of Finance* informed its readers that Marsupial had been a twenty-two-year Ponzi scheme unequalled in the annals of finance (though it would soon get knocked off its perch by Bernie Madoff). From one day to the next its holdings proved utterly worthless. A week later the Bombay stock market saw the biggest collapse in its history, and by month-end the sadhu's curse had come true.

I looked up. A memory was nudging me: of Priti Pinto being told by a financial journalist that they'd started looking into Marsupial. The timing fitted exactly with Samaira's account. As I sat there the sequel struck me as a sort of Shakespearean tragedy, its outcome as inexorable as day and night. After a while I went to the kitchen and warmed up a plate of vegetable curry before taking it to the drawing room and resuming Samaira's letter to the drip-drip of rain against the window.

As you can imagine I kept a low profile on the day I left the country. After checking in with my new fake papers, I bought some magazines and sat down in a dark corner of the airport. That was when I read about Priti Auntie's victory bash complete with a picture of her on Dyalpura's split stairway with the Tiger's Heart reflecting the sunset from her chest. Call me naïve, but she was the last person I'd suspected. Who could have imagined someone stealing their own property? In some ways I have to tip my hat to her for making every detail of her plan come true. Now she sits there, ruling the roost until Duran comes of age.

Or does she?

When Dyalpura fell to the lender bank, they were barred from disposing of it by an inconvenient entity: the Dyalpura Foundation, legal owner of the estate. Before its assets could be touched, the trust would have to be wound down, an onerous and time-consuming process requiring multiple signatures, not least my own. But Priti had it all worked out. Soon after my disappearance she made an appointment at the bank and was ushered into the chairman's office. She had come about the Dyalpura Foundation, she said. Instead of breaking it up it in the hope of an uncertain recovery of the property market, why not sell it to her intact? For good money. The chairman must have gaped. Here was the ultimate godsend, a woman awash with cash and raring to spend it. (Her alimony claim turned out to have been plucked out of thin air.) Brushing off any qualms he might have had as to the legality of her scheme, he shook her hand, and by the end of the meeting they had a deal.

I might have sued them, of course. Far more than just a holding company, our foundation is a set of values specific to one of the oldest royal families in India. As such it cannot just be bought and sold. But where would I have found the lawyers' fees for what would certainly prove the hardest of nuts to crack, all the more so for my having used the trust as collateral for my loans, which made me a de-facto accomplice? In the end I preferred to hammer the final nail in my own coffin by vanishing into the void.

Which brings me to what you once called my disappearing act five months after we met. In those days I was rather lax about things like birth control: after all, you were the first person I'd had sex with in over a year. As a result I paid little heed to my first two missing periods, and when at last I consulted my doctor he declared me to be five months carrying. By now it was far too late to do anything about it, so after vanishing until further notice – anything else would have destroyed my political career – I gave birth to a boy, named him Sanjay after his father and put him up for adoption.

Though you've probably put two and two together, please indulge me for a few more paragraphs. If Priti imagined her purchase of the Dyalpura Foundation to have been aboveboard, she had another thing coming. In particular, she became subject to its bylaws, among them the Article of Succession. 'Should Samaira die without issue,' it says, 'her heir shall be my sister Priti's eldest son Duranjaya.' So far so good. Unfortunately (for her), the prequel is no less explicit: 'Upon Samaira's death she will be succeeded by her eldest son, if she has one' – *which is none other than our very own Sanjay, the eight-year-old boy whose paternity can be ascertained by a DNA test and the details of whose foster parents' are attached.*

One last thing. By common law a missing person is considered dead after seven years of absence, which in my case is April the 1st 2015, twenty-four months hence. On that day Sanjay shall become Maharajah of Dyalpura and sole beneficiary of the Dyalpura Foundation. Neither Priti's scheming nor the passage of time can weaken, let alone avert, this stubborn certainty. My request is that you ensure its application when the time comes. As Sanjay's father and Maharajah of Rajpurwada you have both the right and the standing to do so.

And so goodbye. I have saved enough money to get to the other side of the world, and by the time you read this I shall be six miles high. I hope you will think of me when you look at our child. As for me, as the closest man I ever came to being in love with, you will be in my heart until my dying day.

Samaira

London, April the 9th 2013

I looked up. Before me lay my curry, cold and untouched and uninviting, so I took it to the kitchen and put it back in the fridge. Then I drank a glass of water, turned off the lights and went to my room. As I undressed, my mind jumped to my break-up with Shakti Surnilla. Out of my league, Samaira had called her, and she was right, as time would tell. I was single now, alone but for the odd one-night stand. In my room I remembered Samaira's diamond smile. The thought sparked another: that I would scour the world to find her, and that I would bring her home if it was the last thing I ever did…

# TABLES TURNED

### I

Ever since the tenth century Signora Querini's family had provided Venice with doges, bishops, cardinals, admirals and statesmen of all sorts. Few had as loyally served the Serenissima. Such were Conrad's thoughts as he passed by the Ducal Palace and St Mark's Basilica. The signora proved as kind in person as she was on the telephone, and after shaking his hand with a friendly "*Benvenuto*," she led him towards the apartment he had come to see. Though it was winter and the tourists (relatively) thin on the ground, the spring-to-autumn crush was ever on Conrad's mind. Was it wise to move into the most jam-packed district of the most jam-packed city on earth?

Conrad had often wondered whether to give up on his dream of inhabiting his favourite town due to its impossible tourist crush, or shrug it off and do so anyway. If in the end he had chosen the latter course, it was firstly, and mainly, for the beauty he no longer wished to deprive himself of, and secondly for the back alleys touted by the locals, including Signora Querini, as getaways from the crush. "All you need is to go out and find them," she said. "After that you can roam the city undisturbed." These people had lived here all their lives, he mused, they knew what they were about. While crossing the Ponte Sant' Albano he saw a dark-skinned girl approaching. As she came into focus he noted her lithe body and astonishingly pretty face, like the singer Whitney Houston. When Signora Querini stopped at a wrought-iron gate and fumbled for her keys in her handbag, he fancied that the girl gave him a lingering look before dismissing it as mere wishful thinking.

They stepped onto a quad adorned with the lancet windows that typify Venetian façades. On the left, a front door led them through a derelict entrance to a lift a few steps up on the mezzanine floor. As it heaved into motion the signora told Conrad that the hall was about to be restored, to which he said he didn't mind it as it was, he liked patina, it gave old houses their soul. A moment later she let him into his putative new home. His first thought was for the contrast between his new surroundings and the horrors he'd seen earlier in the day. Having decided against lugging his effects into the notoriously impracticable Floating City, he'd settled on a furnished flat, at least for the time being. (One day he might buy something.) So dire were the interiors he'd been shown that morning, however, so tacky their neo-Baroque furniture, that he'd considered having his belongings shipped over after all. Taking up residence in so stark a contrast to the beauty around him would defeat the purpose of his move – hence his delight at the attractive objects among which he now stood.

Signora Querini showed him around the flat. Its upgrade was now complete, she explained, apart from the curtains and newly upholstered sofas, which would be installed within a few days. Adjoining the living-cum-dining area, two bedrooms flanked an en-suite bathroom with a third to be found up a flight of wooden stairs. In the utilities room a cupboard filled with neatly folded bedclothes and towels stood between a washing machine and a drier. The kitchen, too, was well-equipped. Everything was quietly stylish.

Presently the signora showed him what she called the open-air amenities, starting with the living-room balcony, which gave out onto a jumble of façades, each more beautiful than the last. In summer it would do nicely for breakfast, he said to himself, though at present it was far too cold. Back inside he followed her through the kitchen and up a wooden ladder to what she called the glory of the house. Eagerly he alighted on a roof terrace – and gasped!

From a sea of higgledy-piggledy roofs, all of them fitted with traditional Venetian shingles, church spires rose, near and distant, into the sky: this was the leaning tower of San Giorgio dei Greci, said the signora, this San Pietro di Castello, and that Santi Giovanni e Pietro. As he stood there, a bell tolled two o'clock followed by another and then a third, like an open-air glockenspiel muffled by distance. Apart from that, the sounds of the city were inaudible. Finally the lady turned to him and said, "*Ed ecco il padrone di casa*" ("And this is the host") pointing out the most splendid campanile of all: Saint Mark's, which seemed, by an optical illusion no doubt due to the angle from which he was seeing it, to be rising up from the cupolas of the basilica (though in fact it was an unconnected edifice).

At this point two things dawned on Conrad at the same time: first that he wouldn't find a better place to live; and second that it would slip through his fingers if he dithered. Back indoors he asked Signora Querini to list her conditions – rent, minimum occupancy, termination details, etc., all of which sounded reasonable – and call him in London when she'd met with the other hopefuls. A week later she rang up to say that the flat was his if he wanted it. Repressing his joy, he reserved it as from January 1$^{st}$, by which time he hoped to have received his residence permit from the local authorities.

Beyond his love of the Serenissima, Conrad's decision to leave London stemmed from his very nasty break-up with Claudia. "Marry in haste, repent at leisure," his father had cautioned on his deathbed, as if he'd seen through her even before their marriage. Having borne him no children, her demand of half his fortune "and not a penny less" was a joke and a bad one at that. Not only had they been married for barely eleven months but his money was inherited and she hadn't added a penny to its growth – quite apart from her relapse into her same-sex leanings despite her promise to the contrary. He knew why she hadn't taken him to court: because she didn't stand a chance of prevailing, which hadn't stopped her from bombarding him with emails, all of them threatening, all of them disregarded. If she knew his address, she'd be here now, stalking him to desperation.

In the end it took longer to wrap up his life in London than he'd expected, so he wasn't able to move to Venice till the evening of January 17$^{th}$. The temperature had turned sub-Siberian and the crowds thinned out. Having taken his keys from Signora Querini and dragged his suitcase to his building, he passed its letterboxes – one of which was now captioned Conrad Livingston – and took the lift to the third floor. He began by looking around his new home. Everything was pretty, everything clean and neat and tidy, though he would need to give it a personal touch, hence the throws he'd brought for the sofas in the living room.

His first task was to address a problem that had been needling him for some time: giving his life a purpose now that he was single, friendless and living abroad. Managing his finances wasn't on the cards: most of them were long-term and illiquid and wouldn't keep him busy for more than a couple of hours a week. The same went for sight-seeing: even Zossimo, Signora Querini's "expert in the city's secret landmarks," wouldn't fulfil him in this respect. (Tourism wasn't a job.) His only hope was to fall in love, the ultimate vocation, the only thing worth getting out of bed for. A pity it couldn't be conjured up at will; it either happened or, mostly, it didn't.

He spent his first few weeks looking for the unfrequented alleys of his neighbourhood. Stepping out into the very narrow Calle Sant' Albano, for instance, and turning left, led to the solid throng around St Mark's, while the other way took him to the Rio Santa Cecilia and over its eponymous bridge to the thinly visited Campo Barbarigo. In mid-April, when the temperature started edging up, he would often have breakfast in one of the square's open-air cafés before sallying forth on that day's early-morning jaunt.

During one such expedition he alighted on a little square he didn't know. In front of him two pink palazzi flanked a tenth-century chapel to heart-warming effect. A cluster of children passed by, prattling away on their way to school;

wafts of freshly-ground espresso floated out of the local café; the lilts of Pavarotti's *Santa Lucia* drifted over from a faraway open window. And then, suddenly, like a pack of Pavlov's dogs roused by the toll of nine, the tourists came surging out of every cleft and corner – hundreds of them, thousands of them, pushing and yelling and clicking their phones in their own or each other's faces to the barked injunctions of a baseball-capped guide waving a little flag over her head. Never was romance so fatally slaughtered.

It was at about this time that his loneliness started weighing on him. At first he'd enjoyed its freedom, with no one there to tell him what to do, though at times, during long rainy spells, he would wonder if his vocal chords were atrophying. Then he would open YouTube and hum along to Schubert's Unfinished Symphony, Mozart's 38th, a Chopin nocturne or something by the Beatles or Stones, *The Night Before*, say, or *Carol*. Gradually he began dining out more often in the hope of some alluring encounter. One chilly evening in early April he stepped into Da Lodovico, a well-known restaurant in the district of Rialto. After being asked if he had a reservation and replying in the negative, he was led between busy attendants and guffawing diners to one of only two free tables.

## II

From his place against the far wall he had a clear view of the people waiting to be seated. Visible from behind, a girl in tight blue jeans and a leather jacket was palavering with a waiter at the entrance. At one point she seemed to give the man a tip, and a moment later, as if on cue, he brought her over and asked Conrad if she might join him, for there were no more free tables. Of course, he said, getting up and turning to her. She had curled chestnut hair and light-brown skin and wore small diamond earrings. While wondering why she looked so familiar, he suddenly recognised her as the Whitney Houston lookalike who'd passed him on his first visit to the flat. Before sitting down she took off her leather jacket to reveal full breasts and lean arms emerging from a white tank top. "And so we meet again," he said, holding out his hand for her to shake.

Instead of giving him the quizzical look he'd expected, however, she answered, "And it's all the more of a pleasure."

"You remember me?" he queried disbelievingly while she took her seat.

"Of course," she answered, following suit. "On the Ponte Sant' Albano. You remember *me*, so why wouldn't I remember you?"

He might have rejoined that she was a bronzed beauty of twenty or twenty-one and he a pallid forty-year-old. Instead he asked if she was in Venice by herself.

"I am," she replied, her eyes on him. "And you?"

The question caused him a familiar stirring in the loins. "Me too."

They scanned their menus. Occasionally she might ask him about a dish she didn't know. She had sparkling eyes and a smile that lured one into her aura. When they'd placed their identical orders – granseola followed by cuttlefish with polenta, affogato for pudding and a jug of the house white wine – they discussed each other's families and backgrounds. Her name was Amelia Hurley; she had an Italian mother and a Jamaican father; she spoke decent Italian, lived in south London and worked for a modelling agency that required her regular presence in Venice. When he asked if she knew many people here, she said no, no one at all. At times she'd have dinner with a fellow-model, but mostly she ate in her hotel. "Then why have you made an exception tonight?"

"Because I saw you entering this place and remembered that we'd crossed paths. So I thought we might as well meet."

He smiled. "Flattery will get you everywhere."

She laughed, she had radiant eyes. "Do you live by yourself?" she asked.

"Yes."

"And does it bother you?"

"Being by myself?"

"Yes."

"Sometimes." He leaned back to let the waiter put down his starter. "But generally I like being alone."

Later he paid the bill and followed her out amid cries of *Grazie, arrivederci* from the waiters. In the chill he offered to take her to her *pensione*, the Locanda Casagrande near Campo San Giò, on his way home. When they reached it, she took a selfie with him under the lit-up name of the hotel. His final impression as she waved from the door was the contrast between her diamond earrings and leather jacket. Whatever she wore would look good on her, he thought – which is precisely what models are for.

On St Mark's Square he wondered whether the cathedral's sparkle stemmed from the full moon or his feelings for this girl. Within an hour-and-a-half she'd bewitched him like Circe. Back at the flat he remembered thinking that love was a mission all the more worthy of pursuit for being hard to come by. Was he in love? Time would tell, though the warmth inside him seemed to point that way. In bed he felt himself drifting off to the memory of her last words: that she was flying home in the morning and would get in touch when she returned.

In the weeks to come he gradually succumbed to what he called the underbelly of love, the pain that fills one when the object of one's passion fails to keep her promise: the silent telephone; the claw gripping one's gut; the urge to call her oneself; the crumbling of the self-control that stops one from doing so. Amelia's claim that she knew no one in Venice sounded unlikely: men must flock to her like iron filings to a magnet. Was he mistrusting her already? An old song came to him: "Women seem wicked when you're unwanted…" And then, as he was making to cast off his last vestige of pride and ring her up, she beat him to it.

It was mid-May now, over a month since their dinner, and he'd essentially lost hope – hence his joy when she asked if he was free tonight. Though he had a meeting with Zossimo, the expert in hidden sites recommended by Signora Querini, he decided to move it to the next day. (The guide wanted to tell him about a haunted island in the lagoon but it could wait.) In the hours to come he tried to get online but found the internet down. With a sigh of irritation he folded his computer and vowed to bring it up with Signora Querini if the problem persisted.

Once more they met at Da Lodovico. (This time he'd reserved a table.) Once more she came in a few minutes after him, dispelling his fear that she would stand him up.

And once more she wore her leather jacket, though her tank top had been replaced by a cotton blouse. When she bent down to kiss him, the sight of her cleavage caused him an overpowering surge of lust. Upbeat and bubbly, she bore out the cliché that cheerfulness is among a girl's most alluring traits. When he asked how she'd spent her time in London she said, "With a little help from my friends." Smiling at her reference to an old song, he asked what kind of help, to which she replied that the social season had begun and there'd been weddings and summer parties all over town. "Did you have fun?" he asked.

"At first I did."

"Why at first?"

"Because at the end I got stalked by a crazy lesbian who claimed to be in love with me and wouldn't leave me alone," she said. "That's why I came to Venice early."

"To escape her?"

"Exactly."

"You mean you haven't got any modelling jobs here?"

"Not for ten days," she answered.

"In that case I could take you around town. I've unearthed some less busy neighbourhoods."

"Which ones?"

"Cannaregio; or the Jewish ghetto; or parts of San Polo. Also, there's a mysterious island that I'm going to find out more about tomorrow evening."

She broke into her pretty smile. "It sounds exciting!"

Next morning they met at the fish market, with its assortment of seafood from the Adriatic. When the crush became unbearable they boarded a traghetto to the Ca' d'Oro and followed the Strada Nuova to the

Rio Madonna dell' Orto and the Palazzo Mastelli. After admiring the camel adorning its façade, they crossed the canal and stopped before a rust-red building reminiscent of the city's Byzantine past. "This is Tintoretto's house," said Conrad. "He lived here all his life."

"Wow!" For a moment they admired it in silence. At last she said, "Let's go inside."

"We can't," he answered. "It's privately held and closed to the public."

She smiled. "Then let's have lunch. I'm starving."

The Osteria del Tintoretto had ancient panelling, old wooden tables and a handwritten menu that might have harked back to the artist's day: crostini, legumi alla griglia, pasta al burro, bollito misto and so on. They asked for risotto al pomodoro and the house white wine, ice-cold and slightly metallic. After lunch they headed for the oldest ghetto in the world, its synagogues and kosher restaurants still serving a few Jewish families, before walking to the vaporetto stop of San Marcuola to board a ferry. When she got off at the Accademia Bridge, he kissed her on the cheek with the promise to call her next day. (He couldn't fob off Zossimo again.) Back home he lay down for a siesta and considered his new-found existence. Though his life had now been split into two eras – Before Amelia and After Amelia – he hadn't even made a pass at her, which might be a good thing in that it set him apart from the macho entitlement that can be so off-putting to pretty women, its main victims.

Dinner with Zossimo proved even more interesting than he had expected. "For a century the island of Poveglia served as a quarantine station for those suffering from the plague and other contagious diseases," he began. "Later it became the site of a mental hospital and an old people's home. In 1968 the latter was closed and the island vacated. Believers in the occult claim that Poveglia is the most haunted place in the world," Zossimo concluded. "It is very ... how you say, eerie. But though it is forbidden to outsiders there are ... ways of a getting there."

In the morning Conrad invited Amelia to dinner in his flat and she accepted. After giving her his address, Calle Sant' Albano 4416, he went out to brave the congestion between St Mark's and Rialto. He'd decided to make linguine alle vongole, a local dish whose main ingredient, clams, was to be found at the fish market. Back home he laid the table on the roof terrace before endowing its centre with a string of candles and aligning another along the railing. By the weather forecast, the night would be windless and the temperature fall to a pleasant 21 degrees.

## III

Amelia wore a summer dress that hugged her figure to tantalising effect. Upstairs they sat down on Conrad's newly-acquired wicker armchairs and sipped their Campari-oranges to her eager oohs and aahs. Having visited the Accademia Museum that afternoon, she waxed lyrical about its treasures, from Bellini to Veronese and from Titian to Cima da Conegliano. At regular intervals the toll of a bell came wafting over to dreamy effect. As twilight turned to dusk the windows of the houses below them started lighting up.

It was ten when they came down again, replete and a little tipsy. For a while they sat on the sofa in the room's soft illumination. Briefly Conrad regretted not having any music to soothe the mood before thinking better of it; there was something extraordinarily peaceful about the silence. Outside in the middle distance a couple got up from their terrace and entered their home. Seeing it as a cue, he leaned towards Amelia, slowly so as to let her turn away if she wished, and eased his lips onto hers. So sweet was her reciprocation that he did it again, more confidently this time, more sensually too, her tongue play stirring him to intense arousal.

In his room he lay down on his bed while she rolled a joint at the desk. When she was done she came over and sat down beside him. For a minute they puffed away while the drug intensified the eroticism of the moment. Then she bent down and gave him a long, luscious kiss before sitting up to take another drag. In the process she let him slide his hand inside her blouse and pinch her erect nipples quite hard, which she liked. After a while she undid his flies and returned the favour with long-fingered dexterity…

She was still asleep when he awoke, so he got up and went to brew some coffee in the kitchen. Upon his return he found her washed and dressed; she needed to go to her hotel, she said, sipping at her cup, get ready for the day and check for any emails on her next photoshoots (she never gave her clients her mobile phone number). For lunch he suggested the famous Antiche Carampane near Campo San Polo, and no sooner had he seen her out than he went online to book a table; in the process it struck him that the internet was working again, so he typed her name into Google.

Within seconds he was assailed by a flurry of pictures of "top model Amelia Hurley" wearing a breezy sarong in Bali, a sexy miniskirt in Paris, a skimpy bikini in Copacabana and a sleek winter-sports outfit in St Moritz. He knew the images – God knew it wasn't the first time he'd looked her up – but just as he was about to close the page, the words "An All-Girl Party South Of The River" caught his eye; it was the heading of an article about a recent event in Brixton. The image of two women chatting was captioned in letters too small to make out, so he enlarged it – and gasped. "Amelia Hurley with Claudia Livingston," it said, so he scrolled to the top. "We don't need men," the legend stated. "We have more fun without them."

Amelia was awaiting him when he arrived at the restaurant, so he kissed her on the cheek and sat down. On the wall behind her, variedly-sized mirrors hung in assorted frames; waiters zigzagged around tables covered with crisp white tablecloths. Having placed their orders, they sat back in silence. After a moment she said, "You seem troubled."

There was a long pause. "For good reason," he said at last, nodding slowly.

She kept her eyes on him. Perhaps she foresaw what was coming; no doubt she knew that her picture with Claudia had been posted on the internet. "What reason?" she said at last.

"An All-Girl Party South Of The River." He paused to let her speak but she didn't. "Ring a bell?"

"Of course," she said. "I attended it last week."

"Who were you with?"

"Lots of people." She seemed unfazed. "We must have been sixty or seventy."

"Don't play dumb." Again he paused; again she kept her eyes on him; again it was he who broke the silence. "Who did you go with?" he asked.

"No one. I went by myself."

"And who did you leave the party with?"

"What is this, an interrogation?"

He felt anger rise up inside him. "All right then," he said. "Who were you photographed with at the party?"

"I told you. There were lots—"

"You seem to have trouble answering simple questions. So let me stop beating around the bush. You were pictured with my ex-wife Claudia." He kept his eyes on her. "Am I right?"

"Is that illegal?" she retorted lamely.

Realising that he must roll out the big gun now, he said, "You hang out at a lesbian party with my lesbian wife who's trying to bankrupt me and you act as if it were all in a day's work?"

"Don't be angry, darling." She put her hand on his but he pulled it away. "Please don't."

"If you don't tell me the story, all of it, here and now, I won't just be angry, I shall get up and go."

"Do you want to spoil our lunch?" she said.

"If that's what it takes, yes."

The arrival of their orders put a dampener on their conversation. When the coast was clear Amelia waited for the waiter to fill their glasses. At last she said, "It's true, I went to the party with Claudia. I'd met her before at a similar event. We got on well; she was pretty and fun and easy-going. When I told her I'd just come back from Venice her eyes lit up and she said her ex-husband had moved there.

With sudden intuition I asked her to describe him. It was then that I remembered you on the Ponte Sant' Albano, so I put two and two together and..." She trailed off.

"Go on."

"Remember when I told you I saw you enter Lodovico's and thought we might as well meet?"

He nodded.

"Well that was only partly true. I waited outside your house and followed you to the restaurant so as to find out if my hunch was correct. I even tipped the waiter to get me seated at your table. Later I took a selfie with you outside my hotel, if you recall. Back in London I showed it to Claudia, who confirmed that it was you. 'Conrad's wealth came to him through no merit of his own,' she said. 'There's nothing more reasonable than my request. Half his money is no more than I deserve.' I can't say I agreed with her but I kept it to myself, merely asking why she didn't take you to court, to which she said she no longer needed to, she had a better plan up her sleeve."

At this point the waiter's third attempt to fill their glasses caused Conrad to grab the bottle and snap, "Stop that! Do you think we can't do it ourselves?" As the man scuttled off like a wounded animal, Conrad asked Amelia what Claudia's plan was.

A long silence followed. From time to time she would pick up her fork as if to start on her pasta before putting it down again, her appetite gone the way of his. "To be honest she didn't lay it out right away," she ventured at last. "She said she needed to get it right. After the party in Brixton she wanted to talk to me again, so she called me repeatedly. In the end—"

"Was she the lesbian who claimed to be in love with you?"

"Exactly. In the end I gave in to her persistence to find out the details of her intrigue. So we met again and she told me she'd thought up a scheme to strip you not just of half your money but all of it."

"Is that so?" he answered sarcastically. "And how does she propose to do that?"

"Well … you're still legally married, aren't you?"

"Yes."

"And never had any children."

"No."

"And never made a will, right?"

"Right."

"So by British law she gets everything."

For a while he sat there, shocked at having loved such a fiend. "How sweet," he sneered, "How heart-warming." He paused, briefly. "So what's her plan?"

"Have you heard of a place called Poveglia?" asked Amelia.

"Yes, my guide Zossimo told me about it last night. It's one of Venice's hidden secrets."

"What do you know about it."

"That it's an island opposite the Lido barred to outsiders," he replied before recounting the story of the ships infected by the Black Plague and forbidden from continuing their voyage. "Today much of its surface consists of the ash of 150,000 plague victims cremated on site in the century to come. In the 1920s it was recycled as an insane asylum till its director, crazed with guilt over the forced lobotomies and other experiments he'd inflicted on his already tormented patients, killed himself by jumping off the island's clock tower. For all these reasons Poveglia is held to be the spookiest place in Italy. Given its ban on being visited, it's virtually deserted, which only adds to its mystery." He paused to let her digest the information. "Is that what Claudia told you?"

"More or less. She'd done her homework and decided to use it for her retribution. Unable to do so without a co-conspirator, she saw me as a gift from God or rather Satan. Her plot was simple. When I returned I would get you to fall in love with me. Then I would lure you to Poveglia, which can be done by speedboat under cover of darkness. Once there I would take you up the clock tower on the pretext of admiring the lights of Venice. Then I would push you off it in the belief that your body would never be discovered. When the dust had settled she'd inherit all your money and give me twenty per cent, which is ten million pounds, apparently."

In the silence that followed, Conrad wondered what came next. Amelia's openness about the plot must imply something more. Either she'd refused to act as Claudia's cat's paw or she'd pretended to comply to keep her quiet and find out the details of her plan. In the end he said, "Did you ever intend to join her plot?"

There was a brief silence. "Ten million pounds is a lot of money to me," Amelia replied. "Quite enough to keep me above water for the rest of my life. On the other hand..." She trailed off as if lost for words.

"On the other hand?" Conrad pressed.

"On the other hand I'm not a criminal. Besides..." She trailed off again.

"Besides?"

"There's something more."

"What is it?"

By now her eyes had taken on the glow he was getting to know so well. "That I love you."

IV

Mrs Claudia Livingston
13 Tennant Gardens
London SW7 4DR

Dear Mrs. Livingston,

We have been charged by your husband Conrad to start divorce proceedings in time for his coming remarriage. To stop you drawing out the matter ad infinitum, he has made a will in favour of his future wife. As you know, Anglo-Saxon law allows for the exclusion of anyone from one's will, even one's spouse, all the more so when a couple is in the middle of a divorce.

Please provide me with the name and details of your solicitor so we can forge ahead. As you can imagine, Mr Livingston is anxious to put this matter behind him as quickly as possible.

Thank you and best regards,

Joseph Harrington

Harrington and Walker, Attorneys at Law
17 New Street Square, London EC4

# COINCIDENCE IS FATE

## I

Albi and Naomi Osborn invite you to celebrate
the birth of their seventh child, Rose, at
St Agnes Hall, Cornwall, on
Saturday, December 14th 2024, at 7.30
There will be dinner and dancing
Dress code: '60s cool

Lucas looked up. Though he'd lost touch with the Osborns for a while, they were among his oldest friends. He'd even had a fling with Naomi at university – more than a fling, actually, at least for him. He shook his head. Seven children in twenty-one years! Born in 2004, the eldest, Amber, was old enough to be the youngest's mother. While Albi tried to make ends meet from an artist's studio in Truro, Naomi stayed home to look after their brood. Broke, carefree and universally liked, they were known for their open house and cheap-and-cheerful dinner parties. All night friends and family would drift in and out of the house until the invariably drunken (and usually stoned) small hours. By then the children would have fallen asleep on the couch or some armchair or the carpet in front of the TV. Though they were never put to bed and hardly ever treated to a goodnight story, they were as clever and open-hearted as their parents. There was something Bloomsbury-like about the Osborns' lifestyle. Ten days after receiving their invitation Lucas was heading towards the exit of the Regent's Park tube station when he spotted a familiar figure standing in front of him in the lift. "Albi?" he ventured when they alighted.

The man turned around: it was him, looking unusually tanned. "Lucas!" he exclaimed with a big smile. "What a surprise!" They embraced. "Which way are you going?"

"To the gallery. What about you?"

"Harley Street for a doctor's appointment."

"Nothing serious, I hope," said Lucas as they set off down the Marylebone Road.

"No, no. Just a check-up."

"D'you have one every year?"

"More than one."

Fleetingly he thought of probing that remark before thinking better of it: it would have been tactless. Instead he thanked his friend for inviting him to his celebration.

On the corner of Harley Street they split up with a cheerful "See you at the party." En route towards his workplace Lucas recalled his first meeting with Naomi Tarrant, as she then was. At drinks in one of Oxford Brookes' common rooms, he was sitting on the windowsill when she came up to him. Dusky-skinned and chestnut-haired and sexy, she said she'd noticed him watching her. Today he'd have known how to react – own up to it, pay her a compliment, turn a vice into a virtue – but at the time he blushed and mumbled something silly. "Don't worry," she answered. "I don't mind at all."

"You don't?" he stammered.

"No. Quite the opposite." As if to bear out the remark

she added, "Shall we go to my room for a drink?"

Hardly daring to believe his luck, he answered, "I'd love to."

"Let's leave separately," she said, lowering her voice. "Me first. I don't want any tongue-wagging. My room's in Westminster Hall. Number—"

"I know your room. I've seen you go in and out several times."

With a wink she quipped, "I'm aware."

Many months later, when her love had evaporated, Lucas would recall that conversation as the wellspring of his feelings for her. The thought of being noticed by the uni's crush-girl had stirred him to an upwelling of lust such as he'd seldom known. After a few minutes he left in his turn and made his way to her room. So intense was the upshot, so all-consuming his love, that it changed him forever, if not for better: a few months of delirious happiness ushered in a lifetime of pain. He recalled a line by a Latin-American writer. "To burn with desire and have to keep quiet about it is the biggest misfortune we can bring on ourselves."

If their brief relationship had looked perfect to the outside world, it stemmed largely from her ingenuous stylishness. Seemingly immune from annoyance, her good cheer was constant, her repartee quick and her banter witty. Even when she dumped him for Albi she made it sound like a passing escapade – which did nothing to stem his floods of tears or the claw that gripped his gut when they married. Worse still was the discovery that she'd been two-timing him all along: having wed Albi barely nine weeks after their split-up, she'd delivered Amber seven and a half months later. It didn't take Einstein to work out the chronology.

He crossed the circular garden in the middle of Fitzgerald Square, entered number 3a and took the lift to the second floor. Lucas Stafford Gallery said the plaque on the door; it was 9.30 and he would have half-an-hour to himself. Things were going well for him: apart from his business successes, he'd found a publisher for his short stories. Idly he picked up his book, *Ten Tall Tales by an Art Dealer*, released a month before, and turned to its first chapter, "Tables Turned," which described an incident with one of his artists, Harriet Evans, whose unsolicited advances had caused him to dismiss her from his stable of painters. He recalled her last words as she left the gallery. Turning around with her hand on the door handle, she'd said, "Just you wait."

A week later he was waylaid from a side street and sedated by a rag soaked in chloroform. He awoke in an unknown flat. The conditions imposed by Harriet for his release were that he make love to her whenever she said so; that if she missed her period she would have a pregnancy test and set him free if it was positive; and that if it wasn't, he would have to start again for as long as it took. The problem was that she was short and stocky and over a decade Lucas's senior; that she had bad skin, greasy hair, an ugly face and a nasty smell; and that the only time he got it up thanks to the most potent Viagra pill on the market, which she'd procured for him, she'd scorned his orgasm as premature and said it didn't count.

By now it was three weeks into his capture and he started to despair of ever being liberated. And then, one day while she was out shopping, he saw a man's legs passing the fanlight of the remote basement study he was being kept in. Powerless to open it – being out of reach and blocked from the inside, it could only be unfastened by a blow to its outer framework – he used a ruler to rap on the glass and asked to be rescued. It worked, and fifteen minutes later he was heading for the taxi rank on the corner of Colville Terrace and Westbourne Grove. No sooner had he reached his home than he rang the police.

For various reasons – that no weapon had been used in the kidnapping; that Lucas hadn't been sexually assaulted in the legal sense; and that Harriet had been a first-time offender and pleaded guilty when she was arrested – she got the most lenient sentence in the book, eighteen months, after which she vanished. Luckily the press never picked up on it; nor had he heard from her for two decades, much to his relief. Good riddance!

## II

His drive to St Agnes took five hours. Though it was the eve of the big do, the hall was already teeming with grown-ups and teenagers and children. After showing Lucas to his room, Naomi said there was tea for him downstairs when he was ready. Ten minutes later he entered the library and was handed a cup. Seated all around, young and old were eating fruitcake or ham sandwiches to the sound of the Rolling Stones' *Exile on Main Street*. Still markedly tanned, Albi greeted him with his usual openness. At seven he said he was going to cook dinner and asked if anyone would keep him company. "I'd love to," Lucas shouted out before getting to his feet and following him out of the room. Not for the first time he marvelled at his goodwill towards the man who had killed his happiness; perhaps they were bound by their love for the same woman.

In the kitchen Albi brought two bottles of Tennant's Super Lager out of the fridge and gave one to Lucas, who took a big swig, wiped his lips with the back of his hand and asked how many people were coming to the next day's party. "Two-hundred, give or take," Albi replied.

"Wow! That's a lot! Who's cooking?"

"Me, of course."

"What – for two-hundred people?"

"Sure, why not?"

"What's on the menu?"

"Lasagne."

As they spoke they were joined by the eldest, Amber, looking astonishingly pretty, followed by a blonde boy of about her age, maybe a bit younger. From the cupboard they started bringing out the plates and glasses needed to lay the table in the dining room. There was something ingenuous about them, almost matter-of-fact, as if helping with the kitchen chores was par for the course. Even the boy, who was no blood relation, seemed to know his way around as if it were his home. Meanwhile Albi had put a big vat on the stove and poured in rice and water halfway up. "Risotto?" asked Lucas to a "No, no, nothing so fancy" in return. While waiting for it to boil Albi drizzled some olive oil into a pair of frying pans before emptying two packets of frozen prawns into the now sizzling skillets. "Just a seafood curry," he explained.

At this point the two youngsters came back to fetch some cutlery from a cabinet behind Lucas. The girl gave him a smile that seemed to say, "No offence but you're in the way," so he moved aside and watched her bring out a bunch of knives and forks and spoons and hand them to the boy before picking up another load and following him out. Enchantingly, they seemed to be smiling even when their faces were at rest. Would the syndrome linger into adulthood, or was it an attribute of youth? Later he asked Albi about the boy. "His name's Rory," was the answer. "He's at art school with Amber. I think he's in love with her."

"She's so pretty you can't blame him." He paused while Albi stirred the searing seafood. "Is it reciprocal?"

"I'm beginning to think it is, though he's a couple of years younger."

When the prawns were ready Albi transferred them from the frying pans into the rice. Then he picked up a glass container holding a beige-coloured powder which turned out to be the curry. Delicately he sprinkled it in. "It's home-made," he said, stirring slowly.

"By you?" Lucas asked.

"Yes."

"What's it made of?"

"Cumin seeds, coriander seeds, black mustard seeds, Cayenne pepper, turmeric and a touch of cinnamon."

"Wonderful." A delicious aroma had started filling the kitchen.

All the while Albi was continuing to stir his concoction with a wooden spoon. At last he switched off the hob, washed his hands and said, "Let's go and have a proper drink."

Back in the library he filled two glasses with whisky

and water while a group of new arrivals, none of whom Lucas knew, came swaying in amid loud guffaws. Small talk followed: about the guest list; about the trip down from London; about Christmas and the forecast of snow. Dinner, though no culinary sensation, proved rowdy and fun. The washing-up was done by Albi and his three oldest children (plus Rory) while Naomi joined her guests in the library. (The living room had been emptied to make way for the next day's stage and dance floor.)

At one point she sat down next to Lucas. "It's so nice to see you," she said, her eyes shiny, reminding him of the quip that nothing is as sexy as unfinished business. Though pushing forty, she looked ten years younger – extraordinary after seven children. "Same here," Lucas answered. As so often it struck him that his lack of a family stemmed from his persistent inability to get over his first sweetheart. "I've been thinking of you more often than usual these days," said Naomi suddenly, almost as if she were seeing through him.

He gave her a quizzical look. "How come?"

"Because…" She broke off, her voice wavering, as if unable to finish her train of thought.

"How come?" Lucas repeated.

"Because Albi's … dying."

"*What?*" He felt his blood turn to water. "What d'you mean?"

"Haven't you noticed his skin colour?"

"Yes, I have."

"It's liver cancer."

"Oh my God!"

At the sight of a pair of newcomers Naomi collected

herself and got up with a faux-sprightly "Ah! My favourite people!" for all the world as if she hadn't just revealed the most terrible secret of her life. While she showed them to their room Lucas made himself yet another drink and returned to the sofa. After ten minutes Naomi came back and sat down again. "Please, Luke," she said, using the nickname she'd coined for him at uni, "Mum's the word. Keep it to yourself. You're the only one to know it other than Albi and I."

That night Lucas had trouble falling asleep, his mind awhirl. On the one hand Albi's part in stealing the love of his life hadn't affected their friendship (apart from a few short months at the beginning). He was the nicest man and there'd been no malice in his behaviour. On the other, the inference that his death would allow Lucas to rekindle his own affair with Naomi kept bubbling to the surface. At last he nodded off only to wake up within a couple of hours. Blearily he took a shower, brushed his teeth and swallowed a couple of aspirins. Back in his room he drew the curtains – and gasped. Every tree and meadow and building as far as the horizon was covered in a thick layer of what looked like the fur of a massive polar bear. Smoke curled up from distant cottages; faraway, a car was weaving in and out of the trees like a lone mobile toy.

Downstairs there was no set breakfast; Albi had bought fresh bread and croissants from the local baker before going back to bed. In the kitchen Amber and Rory were helping themselves, so Lucas followed suit. He asked them how old they were and they said twenty for Amber and eighteen for the boy. Behind their open faces they seemed thoughtful, almost grave. After a while Albi came in laden with huge pots and pans and began bustling around the stove. "For a party this size the stage needs to set first thing in the morning," he said.

Lunch consisted of frozen quiches from Tesco's garnished with cheese, vegetables or ham. Albi was busy in the kitchen, so Naomi and her elder children washed up and laid the dinner tables (including the name cards of two-hundred-and-seven guests) with a little help from Rory and Lucas. Visible through the windows, floating snowflakes were lending the landscape a fairy-tale atmosphere. At five Lucas went to his room to catch up on his sleep in time for the party. While shutting the curtains he saw movement below. Visible from behind, a white-haired woman was taking Rory to a run-down old Mini Cooper parked outside the house. After a while it rattled off into the dusk amid Naomi's cry of "Bye, Cosima, see you later" from the main entrance.

### III

It was pitch dark when he awoke. Sounds of jollity were wafting up from the ground floor. He looked at his watch: ten past eight, he'd better get a move on. Having washed in the bathroom across the corridor, he returned to his room and brought his collarless Beatles suit out of the cupboard. Nothing so befitted the party's dress code as the costume first worn by the Fab Four in 1963. When he was done he combed his hair into a mop-top, used an eye liner to thicken his eyebrows and sideburns and gave himself a final look in the mirror.

He found the drinks table set in a corner of the hall amid revellers jostling to make themselves vodkas-on-the-rocks or gins-and-tonic. (There was no barman.) One of them had come as Tom Jones with short curly hair and a goatee; another sported a teddy-boy quiff over a drape jacket and a leopard-skin waistcoat; a gay couple had dressed up as Mick and Keith to surprisingly convincing effect; two or three had come as mods or rockers, dapper suits for the former, jeans and leather for the latter. The girls wore miniskirts, patent-leather boots and beehive hairstyles. Only Albi's bell-bottom pants, gem-encrusted cloak and bushy black sideburns fell flat. ("I wanted to come as Elvis but ended up as *Planet of the Apes!*") Lucas's Beatles suit met with universal approval.

Down and Out had agreed to play for free because their front man was a friend of Albi's. At midnight they were intoning their last number, *The Devil's Own*, when Lucas stepped out into the garden and lit a cigarette. While ambling through the snow he came upon a coppice of trees standing guard by a gap in the hedge that led to a beach fifty yards beyond. Lit up by the moon's pallor, a couple was standing among the trees. It was Amber and Rory locked in a passionate embrace.

After a tactful retreat Lucas circled the house and re-entered the living room through the French window. The band had now been replaced by an Afro-Cuban playlist. A few of the guests had gone to bed; those who remained were clearly the worse for wear. Suddenly he caught sight of Naomi sitting all alone by the embers of the fire. On a whim he joined her. "You'll never guess who I spotted in the garden," he said.

She turned to him with a drunken air. "Amber and Rory?"

"Yes. How did you know?"

She shrugged. "Because I saw them sneak out of the house earlier."

"Did—"

"And because they're in love."

"They are?"

She nodded slowly.

"Since when?"

"I don't know, a year."

There was a pause while the fire crackled away. "And do you approve?"

"Of course I do. I love them both. Rory's mother's a bit of a crackpot but her son's the sweetest thing."

"Who is—"

"But there's something else, something I've been meaning to tell you for twenty years."

"Sounds ominous."

"Amber's your daughter," she said, ignoring his remark.

"*What?*" He turned to her with furrowed brow; he must have misunderstood. "What are you talking about?" he said.

"Which part of 'Amber's your daughter' don't you get?"

There was a drunken pause. "How do you know?" he probed, his mind befuddled.

"Because I was nine weeks pregnant when I married Albi and hadn't had sex with anyone else for at least six months."

At this point a stranger darkened the doorway. "I've come to collect Rory," he said in a thick Cornish accent.

"Truro Taxis?" she asked.

"That's right."

"I think he's in the library. Let me get him for you. I'll bring him to the entrance hall."

For a long time Lucas stared into the dying fire. After a while, too drunk to fathom the meaning of what he'd just learned, he got up and took the back stairway to the second floor. In his room he drank an Alka Selzer and went to bed. If Amber was really his daughter common decency would require him to contribute to her upkeep. In the almost certain event that Albi's days were numbered, it would be unconscionable to leave Naomi to fend for herself with barely a penny to her name.

## IV

Held in Truro, Albi's funeral was limited to his closest family circle: the deceased's parents and Naomi's plus their children and a couple of aunts and uncles: no cousins or nieces, no nephews or close friends, all of whom were invited to a memorial service at London's Brompton Oratory a month later. It was a sad affair given Albi's popularity and relative youth. At the wake, held in a nearby hotel, Lucas asked Naomi how long she planned to stay in London. Forty-eight hours, she replied, so he suggested dinner the next day and she accepted. At the Locanda Parmigiana they placed their orders; while the waiter made his way to the kitchen Lucas turned to her and said, "I want you to know that I'm here for you." To put her mind at rest for what must have been her most pressing concern, he added, "Both financially and otherwise."

"Thank you, darling," she said, putting her hand on his. "You don't know the weight you're taking off my shoulders. I was even thinking of selling the Hall."

"Don't do that. It would be awful to deprive the children of their childhood home."

She nodded tearfully. After a brief pause she suddenly said, "Amber and Rory have decided to get married."

"*What?*" He looked at her incredulously. "But..." – he shook his head – "Is it even legal?"

"The minimum age for marriage without parental consent is eighteen. And they're both past that age – though barely, in Rory's case."

He asked if she'd tried to stop them.

"Oh yes," she replied. "To no effect, of course. Nothing is as hard-headed as first love."

Lucas shrugged. There seemed nothing for it but to relent and hope for the best. All they had was parental pressure without even the support of the law.

A day or two later he was about to go to work when the postman brought him a letter marked St Agnes, Cornwall. He slit it open and read the following.

Dear Lucas,

The reason I didn't attend the Osborns' party was the sight of your name on the guest list. So forbidding is the news I need to tell you that I wanted to do it in writing and in less frivolous conditions. Until a while ago I wasn't sure when to tell you the truth, but a recent development has forced my hand.

First of all let me explain my movements after being released from jail. Unwilling to stay on at the site of my misbehaviour, I moved to Cornwall in search of anonymity. It is many miles from London and most of its villages are remote and unknown, including St Agnes. The only time strangers come to town is when the Osborns host some social event. Eager to seal my status as a complete unknown thanks to the press's ignorance of my crime, I decided to drop my first name and use the second, Cosima. For eighteen years all went well. But this has now changed. Rory has decided to marry Amber Osborn, so I have no other choice than to bare the truth.

My conditions when I held you captive in the basement of my Notting Hill flat – that I wouldn't set you free till you got me pregnant – seemed to all intents and purposes never to have been met. Nor did I seek any kind of medical opinion after your escape: why bother? But when I missed my next two periods I asked to see the prison gynaecologist and found out that your premature orgasm had had an unanticipated outcome. Six months later Rory was born in Holloway Jail. Hence this letter, which I am sending under intense strain: the only hope of preventing our son's impulsive decision to marry so young is for the two of us to block it together. Naomi agrees, so I suggest we put collective pressure on them to reconsider. It is our only hope.

With love,

Harriet

Lucas looked up. The news harboured something too ominous to ignore. When at last it sank in, he went online and found out that matrimony between half-siblings was illegal. "If they marry anyway, the union will be automatically void, even if they don't know they are related." For a while he sat there with a leaden weight in his stomach; when at last he collected himself he knew what he had to do. First, establish the lovers' blood bond by DNA; second, inform them of the outcome; finally, if all else failed, rope in the law. He shook his head. A fine way to rekindle his first love by subjecting both his children to the heartache he had himself endured for the last twenty years...

# Acknowledgements

Sincerest thanks to my editor, Beena Kamlani, for teaching me how to write; to my publisher, Sam, for his patience and enthusiasm; and to all those who helped me in the research for these stories.